Sock

Other books in the series

Thumb
Ouch!
Pigeon

One Weird Day at
FREEKHAM HIGH
Sock

Steve Cole

OXFORD
UNIVERSITY PRESS

OXFORD
UNIVERSITY PRESS

Great Clarendon Street, Oxford OX2 6DP

Oxford University Press is a department of the University of Oxford.
It furthers the University's objective of excellence in research, scholarship,
and education by publishing worldwide in

Oxford New York

Auckland Cape Town Dar es Salaam Hong Kong Karachi
Kuala Lumpur Madrid Melbourne Mexico City Nairobi
New Delhi Shanghai Taipei Toronto

With offices in

Argentina Austria Brazil Chile Czech Republic France Greece
Guatemala Hungary Italy Japan Poland Portugal Singapore
South Korea Switzerland Thailand Turkey Ukraine Vietnam

Oxford is a registered trade mark of Oxford University Press
in the UK and in certain other countries

British Library Cataloguing in Publication Data

Data available

ISBN-10: 0-19-275425-4
ISBN-13: 978-0-19-275425-7

1 3 5 7 9 10 8 6 4 2

Typeset by Palimpsest Book Production Limited,
Polmont, Stirlingshire

Printed by Cox & Wyman Ltd, Reading, Berkshire

For Justin Richards—firm friend
and partner in crime

Registration

Classroom plus thirty pupils minus teacher equals NOISE. At least, that was the way the maths worked in most of the schools Sara Knot had attended.

Freekham High, she reflected, was *not* most schools.

This morning there was no laughter, no chatter, no running about or paper fights. Nothing. The class had gathered in awed silence around quiet, freckle-faced Ginger Mutton.

It was weird, this business about Ginger. If Sara was feeling unkind—which she wasn't usually—she might say that Ginger was a bit of a dweeb. Small and a bit pathetic-looking, Ginger always slouched because her uniform was too small for her. Her copper-bright hair was lank, and her fringe flopped down below a tatty headband. She wore deeply uncool chunky-frame

 1

glasses that magnified her eyes to the size of saucers.

In any other school, Ginger would be the kind to sit quietly at the back in a little world of her own, underachieving and overlooked.

But, again, Freekham High was *not* like any other school.

And Ginger was not like any ordinary dweeb.

She had found a secret weapon. And she'd used it to force her way into the hottest cliques in school.

Right now Ginger sat cross-legged on a table, staring around at her enthralled classmates. It was only really Sara and her best mate, Memphis Ball, who were hanging back.

'I must concentrate,' Ginger announced in a spooky whisper, swaying her head from side to side. 'Mystic messages are starting to form . . . '

Excited mutterings ran through the classroom.

'Hurry up,' someone hissed. 'Mr Penter will be back in a minute to take the register!'

'Yeah, come on, Mutton!'

Ginger glanced at the clock above the chalk-board. 'It is not *I* who may speak the messages,' she reminded them, raising her right hand in the air. 'It is . . . Big Stitch!'

 2

'Her *sock*,' said Sara, her long blonde hair trailing about her shoulders as she shook her head despairingly. 'Look at her, Memphis! Ginger's got practically the whole class eating out of her hand—because she's wearing a sock on it!'

'Eeuw!' Memphis pulled a face. 'Eating out of a sock, nice thought!' A trim, wiry girl with a shaved head and amazing green eyes, Memphis was kind of kooky but cool. She seemed to know almost everyone in the school, which made her an expert on who was hot and who was not. This was handy for a new girl like Sara, who'd only started at Freekham two weeks ago.

Ginger Mutton had gone from zero to hero in the same stretch of time. And it was all thanks to Big Stitch, the sock puppet she brandished on her right hand—a woolly, mad-looking bundle of patches and stripes. Two buttons, one bigger than the other, formed its eyes. An embroidered square of material made the nose. A finger snipped from a glove was poked inside its 'mouth' to make a lolling tongue.

'The mists are beginning to clear,' Ginger intoned. 'Who will dare to bare their soul to his sole?'

 3

'Me!' 'I will!' The cries rose up. 'Speak to us, great sock!'

Sara saw that only Thomas Doughty was taking no notice. Broad, blond, and bushy eyebrowed, he sat with his back to the throng.

'Doubting Thomas is the biggest sceptic in school,' Memphis observed. 'He doesn't believe in anything unless it involves sports—a hand-stitched sock doesn't stand a chance!'

But Thomas was in the minority. Big Stitch held the rest of the class in the palm of his . . . Well. In the sole of his foot, anyway.

Here was a piece of footwear with special talents.

According to Ginger, Big Stitch could tell the future.

At first, people had laughed at this funny little girl running around making predictions. They would cruelly mock the sock and tell her to get lost.

But then the predictions started to come true.

'Now I shall call upon the sock of ages,' said Ginger in a high wavery voice. 'I shall ask him to tell us that which is yet to be . . . '

'Well, *I'm* yet to be convinced,' said Sara flatly.

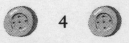

'You have to admit,' said Memphis, 'that sock's got a good track record. It predicted that Cassie Shaw would find happiness with a pigeon, and everyone laughed. But then John Pidgin in the Lower Sixth asked her out the next day! Now they're in *lurrrve*.'

'Could be total coincidence,' Sara argued.

'But Ginger's brought five cool couples together in the last ten days!'

'They probably had the hots for each other anyway.'

'OK, then,' Memphis argued, 'what about when Big Stitch told Mrs Hurst's year ten netball team they'd enjoy a brief victory last Thursday?'

'They lost!'

'True. But to cheer them up afterwards, the Games teacher told them they could wear their own knickers during matches from now on instead of those nasty scratchy PE ones! That's a *briefs* victory, if nothing else! And what about—'

She broke off as Ginger cried out: 'I urge you to speak to us now, Big Stitch, as I recite the rhyme of time!'

The sock was swaying madly like a loopy cobra getting ready to strike.

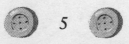

'Here we go,' Memphis murmured 'She's summoning the sock spirit!'

While the puppet fixed the audience with its wonky stare, Ginger began to chant:

> 'Big Stitch, Big Stitch, soft, snug, and
> wool-rich,
> Show us a future idyllic.
> Your toe's in the know and your heel
> shall reveal
> Even though ten per cent is acrylic!'

The sock stiffened. Its mouth gaped open.

'Sam would be loving this,' hissed Sara. 'Wonder where he is?'

Memphis shrugged. 'Late again. Third time this week.'

'And it's only Wednesday.' Sara smiled.

Thinking of Sam Innocent usually made her smile. He was infuriating in many ways—cheeky, stubborn, refusing to take anything too seriously—but the two of them shared a curious kind of bond.

They had both been born at the same time on the very same day: February 29th. Weird.

Both had parents with low boredom thresholds, so they'd each spent most of their thirteen years

 6

moving house and switching school. Three times last year, and twice more since. *Spooky* weird.

And they'd both started at Freekham High on the very same day in the middle of May—just in time to get dragged into a bizarre mystery involving a lot of severed thumbs and fingers. *GROSS!*

It was as if they were living magnets attracting weird stuff or something.

Or maybe it was something about Freekham High itself . . .

A high-pitched squawk seemed to burst from Big Stitch.

'I have a message for Thomas Doughty!' the sock said. Ginger was a good ventriloquist. Only if you looked closely could you see her lips moving.

Thomas looked back over his shoulder. 'Give it a rest, Mutton!'

'Misfortune is coming your way,' said the sock in its funny voice. 'Beware the full moon, Thomas! Beware the fall of the full moon!'

'Yeah, right,' said Thomas. 'That's a talking sock and you're a ginger. Why should I believe either of you?'

The sock shook as if it was laughing 'I was right before, wasn't I?'

'That's true,' said Memphis. 'It said Thomas would be lucky in love . . . '

'Yeah, I know—he found a fiver under his desk when we looked at *Romeo and Juliet* in English,' said Sara. 'What does that prove?'

'Well, what about when Big Stitch warned him that trouble was afoot?' Memphis argued. 'It turned out to be a *left* foot—he lost one of his new trainers in the changing rooms! Hey, you should ask the sock about that bracelet you lost last week. You've looked everywhere and you can't find it.'

'Don't remind me. I think my dad accidentally threw it out with the garbage,' Sara grumbled. 'Memphis, are you trying to tell me you *really* believe in a soothsaying sock?'

She shrugged. 'I'm keeping an open mind. Since you and Sam showed up at Freekham, I'm ready to believe pretty much anything!'

'Where *is* Sam?' wondered Sara. 'He's *really* late this morning.'

'Hey, Stitch,' called Fido Tennant, cool kid in class with a thatch of brown hair and a winning

 8

smile. His real name was Dorian, so he found his nickname a big improvement. 'Tell me straight—am I going to win my races in Sports Day this afternoon?'

Sara listened in. She was running in the girls' hurdles and the 1500 metres herself, and Mrs Hurst the Games teacher said she was a strong contender to win. Even so, Sara didn't like to count her chickens before they hatched.

Ginger was giving nothing away. 'You know that Big Stitch will not answer direct questions,' she said. 'He only makes his own predictions.'

Fido shrugged. 'Well, I just thought that since he's a sock he might appreciate a question that involved running shoes.'

Big Stitch twitched on the end of Ginger's arm. 'I have a prediction to make about *you*, Fido,' it said in its strange, sockish manner. 'You will get your geography homework back today—'

'Duh!' said Thomas. 'What kind of prediction is that? We've got Geography second period, we'll *all* get our homework back!'

The sock shook its head sagely. 'But Fido will get a rubbish mark! The worst in the whole class!'

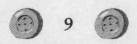

At this, Fido frowned. 'But that essay was easy!'

'Ha, ha,' laughed Ruth 'Ruthless' Cook—to whom being mean came as easy as breathing. 'Serves you right, you swot.'

'Silence!' cried Big Stitch—and miraculously, Ruthless obeyed. 'Another message is coming to me from the future . . . An important message for . . . Vicki Starling!'

'For me?' gasped Vicki. 'Wow!'

Sara rolled her eyes at Memphis. Vicki was the crowned queen of the year's A-crowd. Her blue eyes, dimpled cheeks, and platinum blonde bunches were to die for—trouble was, she knew it. Her circle of prom queen wannabes—Denise, Elise, and Therese, the so-called Chic Clique—basked in Vicki's reflected glory, always trying to outdo each other in their quest to be her best buddy. Sara watched them now as they fell about gasping and giggling in frenzied excitement until the Sock shushed them sternly into silence.

Ginger glanced at her watch, and Sara saw that registration was almost over. Surely Penter would be here any time now?

'Vicki,' said the sock gravely, 'you are destined

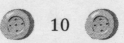

to find true love with *the very next person to walk through the classroom door!*'

'Oh my God!' Vicki squealed, amid a bunch of ear-splitting shrieks from her clone club. 'Love! Can it be true?'

'Of course it can't be true,' sneered Doubting Thomas.

But the whole class fell silent in any case, eagerly watching the door. The clone club held its collective breath. Even cynical Sara couldn't tear her gaze away.

'Let's hope it's not Penter!' she whispered.

Memphis grinned. 'If it is, that's one sick sock!'

Then, suddenly, the door flew open.

And Sam Innocent came racing inside.

A giant gasp went up at the sight of him. Memphis and Sara swapped startled looks. Ginger looked pretty amazed too. She looked at the sock accusingly as if it had been holding out on her.

'Vicki, it's *Sam!*' cried Therese, as if no one had actually noticed.

'*Him?*' Vicki stared in disbelief.

'Gotta go,' squawked Big Stitch quickly, as Ginger unrolled the sock from her wrist.

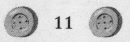

'Sorry I'm late, I . . .' Sam tailed off as he took in the incredulous faces all staring his way. He'd been running—his freckled cheeks were flushed red, his dark spiky fringe plastered to his forehead with sweat. 'Where's Penter?' he panted. 'Did I rush all the way here for nothing?'

Vicki turned on Ginger. '*That* is meant to be my true love?'

Scandalized whispers started up around the class.

'Well played, mate!' called Fido, giving Sam a thumbs-up.

'Unlucky, Starling,' sniggered Ruthless Cook.

'What's going on?' said Sam. Then he noticed Ginger—or rather, the woollen bundle in her hand, and he groaned. 'Don't tell me that stupid sock has been reading the tea-leaves again.'

'Yep,' called Sara. 'And it says that you're going to be Vicki Starling's ickle darling!'

Sam's jaw dropped amid wolf-whistles and jeers and more laughter. Doubting Thomas shook his head as if it was all beneath him. Vicki's friends started queuing up to give Vicki wet little embraces.

But from the look of shock on Vicki's face,

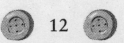 12

Sara wasn't sure if they were congratulating her or giving her pity.

'Cheek of her!' complained Sara. 'Acting like Sam's way beneath her.'

Memphis raised an eyebrow. 'Jealous?'

'No way!' Sara protested, blushing. 'I'm just saying—'

But the next moment, the imposing figure of Mr Penter marched in and all chatter ceased. The class swiftly dispersed to their usual places around the room.

'I should hope so, too!' growled Penter. His hair had been carefully combed with obsessive neatness, but his red-rimmed eyes and patchy beard undid the good work; left him looking more like some clapped-out rabid animal in a wig. 'I've just been checking arrangements for this afternoon's Sports Day with Mrs Hurst. I think you should know that my form has come in the top three overall for each of the last ten years. And to ensure that this record shall continue, rest assured I shall be involving myself very closely.'

'Are *you* running in a race then, sir?' asked Fido innocently, to much laughter. It was the sort

 13

of dumb line that Sam might have come out with—but Sara could see he was too busy glaring at Ginger to be cheeky to anyone.

She also saw that Vicki Starling was watching him from across the classroom, thoughtfully.

Period One
Maths

Usually, when the school siren sounded the start of first period, Sam was first out, revelling in his few minutes of freedom between one classroom and the next. But now he hung back and let others go before him. He knew the jokes and teasing he was in for and he could live without them.

He had nothing against Vicki Starling. He supposed a lot of blokes must dream of being put in the frame as possible boyf material. But the only words Sam had ever said to her were 'Whoops!' when he accidentally bumped into her one time, and 'Ouch!' when she'd trodden on his foot to get her own back. She barely knew he was alive. If she wanted to get to know him better, well, that was fine—but if it took a patchwork sock to persuade her, she could push off.

Besides, Vicki was way out of his league and he knew it. He would never be able to relax

  15

around her. She was more of a sleek lioness than a Starling, while he was the equivalent of a rangy hyena. But that was OK. Hyenas skulked about having a laugh, eating loads of food and annoying people. They could even turn their bums inside out, which in Sam's books was pretty impressive. All lionesses did was sit around preening in between snacks—and he had no wish to find himself on the menu.

He noticed Sara coming up to him, her blonde hair pouring over her shoulders, wide blue eyes sparkling with amusement. She folded her arms. 'Hey, studmuffin! How come you're not walking out hand in hand with Vicki—playing hard to get?'

'Leave it,' Sam warned her.

She gave a slightly horsy snicker. 'Why were you so late, anyway? Beating off screaming girls? Or secret, last minute training for Sports Day?'

'You know I didn't qualify in the heats,' he said.

'Yeah, because you didn't want to. So why *were* you late?'

'Actually, I had an accident.'

Her face clouded. 'Are you OK?'

'I guess.'

'What happened?'

Sam grinned. 'I accidentally couldn't stop watching TV after breakfast.'

Sara pulled a face. 'Ha, ha. Are you coming to maths, or what?'

'Sure. But first, I've got to find a moth and catch it.'

'A *moth*?'

'Uh-huh. I'm going to put it in Ginger Mutton's bag and hope it chews a hole in that stupid big-mouthed sock of hers.'

'Won't make any difference. Vicki thinks it's telling the *hole* truth already.'

'Lame!' Sam groaned. 'Sara, all this guff about fortune-telling socks . . . *You* don't believe Ginger's got second sight, do you?'

'Well, if anyone does, she does.'

'*What?*'

'Stands to reason—her glasses are twice as thick as anyone else's!' she teased. 'See ya!'

Sara hurried along the science block's gleaming corridor. Freekham was an ugly, modern school—all glass and steel buildings and concrete walkways, sharp angles and low ceilings. But it was built on a very old site. It seemed to Sara that sometimes, among the everyday school whiffs of chalk dust, gym shoes, and disinfectant there was a trace of some other smell that clung on, out of time. A smell of must and wood smoke and maybe sulphur; a *weird* kind of a smell.

A hundred years ago, the school and its grounds had been the site of a lunatic asylum that burnt to the ground. And a hundred years before *that*, an old government building stood here—until it was struck by lightning and blown to bits.

Somehow, Freekham High had become a place where weird stuff went to happen.

Sara was just turning out of the science block on her way to the maths building when she noticed none other than Ginger Mutton ahead of her. She was talking to an older boy, burly and surly with a square jaw and piggy eyes. Or rather, *he* was talking *at* her. And neither of them seemed very happy.

Sara knew it was none of her business. But then, this guy *was* about twice Ginger's height.

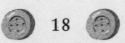

She quickened her step. 'Everything OK, Ginger?'

Ginger saw her and slumped with relief. 'Oh, I'm fine, thanks!' she said, looking nervously up at the sour-faced boy. 'I was . . . I mean, we were just . . .'

The boy gave Sara a filthy look, then skulked off towards the science block without another word.

'Who's that little bundle of sunshine?' asked Sara.

'Carl Witlow,' Ginger sighed. 'It's nothing. Since Big Stitch took off, people keep hassling us to predict their future, to tell them what's going to happen.' She bit her lip. 'And sometimes it's not something they want to hear.'

'That's the way the fortune cookie crumbles, I suppose,' Sara shrugged. 'Doesn't it bother you, though? Gorillas like him coming on all stroppy?'

'I wasn't worried that time,' Ginger confided. 'I knew *you'd* come along.'

'You did? How?'

'Big Stitch told me, of course.' With that, she patted her sports bag and ran off down the corridor. 'This sock rocks!'

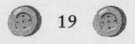

Sara shook her head in bafflement. Then Sam sidled up beside her.

'You heard that?' she asked.

'Heard what?'

'Ginger really believes in that sock stuff. I thought it was just some game she was playing at first . . . but she actually does take it seriously.'

'Maybe because when she puts Big Stitch on her wrist, people take *her* seriously,' Sam suggested.

'But it's just a sock! How can they!'

'Do you read your horoscopes in the papers, or in magazines?' he asked her.

'Well, yeah.'

'And do you take them seriously?'

'Sometimes, I guess,' said Sara. 'But that's different! Those are written by *real* astrologers!'

'Oh yeah?' Sam smiled mischievously. 'How do you know they're not getting their sock puppets to do all the work for them?'

'I thought you didn't believe in Big Stitch?'

'I don't. But I believe in winding you up.'

She scowled. 'We'll be late for Maths.'

'Is that another prediction?'

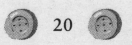

'It's a fact!' She grabbed him by the ear and pulled him along after her. 'So come on!'

As soon as Sam walked into the class the Chic Clique burst out in giggles and whispers and Vicki Starling blushed. She hadn't looked at him twice in the last fortnight, and now suddenly he was the centre of attention—and all on a sock's say-so.

Sara went off to sit beside Memphis, leaving Sam to take the only other spare chair—right next to Ashley Lamb. Nice one. Ashley was an ex-geek struggling along the road to rehabilitation. But he'd only recently stopped sucking his thumb, so he had a long way to go.

Sam heard the Chic Clique talking in too-loud whispers behind him.

'I just couldn't believe it when Sam Innocent walked through that door!' hissed Denise.

'It's like that fairy story about the princess and the woodcutter,' said Elise. '*They* found true love— even though he had no social status whatever.'

'Remember, Vicki, the sock was right about Cassie and John,' said Therese, swooning.

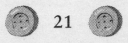 21

'And Kirsten and Mike,' added Denise. 'And Jenny and Rob, too!'

'It's *totally* your fate, Vicki,' Elise declared.

'I was going to say that,' Therese complained.

'I wish they'd all just put a sock in it,' sighed Sam.

'Girls like that are bad news,' said Ashley suddenly, a philosophical look on his baby face. 'They start out smiling and nice . . . but once they get their teeth into you, you're finished!'

Sam frowned at him. 'What would you know about it, Ashley? The only female who ever smiled at you was your mum!'

'And even then, only when I fell over!' Ashley agreed. 'But I still reckon that girls like that are bad news. I just know it.'

Sam nodded. 'I don't need you *or* a fortune-telling sock to tell me that!'

Just then, Mr McLennon—the pathetically eager maths teacher—flapped into the room, absentmindedly patting his head. He had gone very thin on top, and the few strands of hair he used to try and cover his bald patch always wound up waving about like mini aerials.

'Hello, m'friends,' he said brightly, his smile

as watery as his blue eyes. 'Let's not waste time, we've got a lot to get through today—we're looking at probability theory . . . '

'What's the probability it's totally boring,' sighed Sam.

As if in agreement, the girls went on whispering behind him.

'Now, probability theory is all to do with the likelihood of a particular event occurring . . . '

Sara looked across at Ginger Mutton while McLennon spouted on. What was the probability of a girl like her ending up so much in demand? She bet that even Big Stitch couldn't have foretold how trendy his mistress would become as a result of his so-called prophecies.

Well, Sara decided, the two of them could feel proud of the work they'd done today. At the next table, Vicki Starling was still going on about her supposed new love.

'Do try to pay attention, Vicki,' called McLennon.

'Sorry, sir,' she answered with a flutter of eyelashes and a smile.

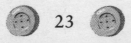 23

'Oh, that's all right,' said McLennon cheerfully.

He turned back to the chalkboard while Vicki turned straight back to Therese beside her.

'See, when I saw Sam walk in, I was, like, completely freaked out.'

'Freaked out, uh-huh,' said Therese, wearing her most understanding expression—which since she didn't understand much besides eyelash curlers and lip-gloss, wasn't saying much.

'But you know, I think I'm slowly coming to terms with it,' Vicki explained. 'It's like, Big Stitch has made up my mind for me, right?'

'Made up, totally,' Therese agreed.

'And there are just so many guys crazy about me! Richard, Amjit, Justin . . . And what about that psycho in the year above—I mean, hello!'

Dopey Therese grinned with delight. 'Oh, hi, Vicki!'

'When you can have anyone you want, who do you choose?' Vicki's smooth forehead puckered with perfectly straight worry lines. 'It's just *so* tough!'

'Not as tough as having to listen to this garbage!' said Sara through gritted teeth. 'If she doesn't shut up soon, the probability I'll be sick is *very* high.'

'Snap,' said Memphis miserably.

For once, Sara tried her best to focus on McLennon's boring lesson. While she'd always felt that maths was strictly for the birds, it beat the hell out of listening to twittering Starlings.

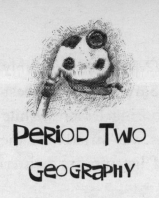

PERioD Two
GeoGRapHy

The hooter sounded the end of Maths, cutting short McLennon's lecture about which side a flipped coin was most likely to land on, head or tails. As the class packed away their stuff, Sam reflected that any coin flipped at Freekham would most likely land on its edge. Things had never been so freaky at the other schools he'd been to; but then, at least the days were rarely dull.

Only weird.

He fell in with Memphis and Sara as they all filed out of the classroom, making for the humanities block.

'I ought to sue you for damage to my ears,' grumped Sara.

Sam frowned. 'Me?'

'Yeah, *I* ought to sue you too,' said Memphis. 'Sam, if you hadn't walked through that door when you did, then Icky Vicki would be safely

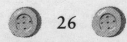 26

out the way in the sick bay throwing up at the thought of marrying Penter—and we wouldn't have to put up with her going on about her love life!'

'I hear what you're saying,' said Sam. 'And I think it's time I nipped this in the bud!'

The three of them could clearly hear Vicki and her Chic Clique gassing on in a huddle ahead.

'I know the sock has been right about everyone else, but . . . Sam Innocent!' Vicki sighed. 'It does take some getting used to. He's *so* immature!'

'Maybe it's just an act he puts on,' said Elise.

'To hide his true feelings!' gasped Therese.

And Denise agreed. 'It's so you won't know he's dying for your love!'

'No, actually, I *am* just immature,' said Sam, pushing through their little throng and making a fart noise with his palms to stress the fact. 'I'm revolting. I'm vile.' He stuffed two fingers up his nose and had a good rummage. 'See? And you don't even want to know what else I've been picking with these fingers,' he said, sticking them in his mouth for good measure.

'I'm out of here,' said Vicki, repulsed.

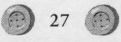

27

As she stalked away, Sam looked back at Sara and Memphis and winked.

Elise, Therese, and Denise glared at him in disgust for a moment.

Then Elise nodded to the others. 'You know, girls, that is *so* an act.'

'He's *totally* into her!' beamed Therese.

'He's just shy!' said Denise. 'Afraid of his own feelings.'

'I'm sure Vicki will forgive you,' Elise assured him. 'It's, like, your destiny.'

And they all went off happy, leaving Sam muttering darkly in their wake.

'Nice try,' said Sara. 'Now wash your hands.'

Sam surveyed his sticky fingers. 'I guess I should. See you in Killer Collier's class.'

He detoured off to the cloakrooms, which were filled with people dawdling on their way to lessons, and passed Thomas Doughty coming out of the Gents.

A second later, Thomas yelled in alarm and went crashing.

Sam spun round. Thomas was lying sprawled on his back in the cloaks, clutching his ankle. Jackets and bags had tumbled all around.

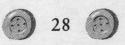

'What happened?' asked Sam, crouching beside him. 'What did you do?'

'Slipped on something,' Thomas muttered through gritted teeth.

'Soap!' said Sam, helping him to stand. He pointed to a pasty white bar on the floor beside a large black bag. 'You slipped on a bar of soap!'

Thomas tried to walk, and Sam grabbed him before he could fall back down again. 'I can't put any weight on my ankle!' groaned Thomas. 'It's Sports Day this afternoon—what am I going to do?'

'I'd say you were out of the running,' said Sam. 'And probably every other event, too.'

A small crowd had gathered round them—not to try and help Thomas, of course, just to gawp at the fact he'd fallen.

'Big Stitch *said* that bad luck would befall him!' gasped mousy Michelle Harris.

'Another prophecy come true,' Ashley declared.

'Rubbish!' Thomas cried. 'Ginger spouted some junk about a full moon. And in case you hadn't noticed, it's broad daylight!'

But Sam felt a shiver run through him as he

spotted something in the pile of blazers and bags on the floor. 'Uh, Thomas?'

He held up a black sports bag. On one side of it, as part of a band's logo, was a fat yellow full moon.

'You must have knocked it when you fell,' said Sam.

'Beware the fall of the full moon!' squeaked Michelle Harris. 'That's amazing! Wait till Ginger hears about this!'

She turned and ran off in the direction of the geography classroom, leading the crowd in an excited charge.

'What did you have to show them *that* for?' grumped Thomas.

'Well, you have to admit, it *is* pretty weird,' said Sam, hanging the bag back up.

The full moon looked like a big yellow eye. Sam could almost imagine it staring after him as he helped Thomas limp along the corridor towards Geography.

When Sara came into the classroom, she found that Ginger was at it again. With one hand up

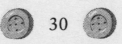

Big Stitch's unmentionable, she seemed cool and confident as she spoke to the rest of the class, a far cry from her usual nervous self.

'The snack bar will run out of Big Chunx bars today,' she said, the sock's lips moving while her own remained still. 'Get in quick and you'll be lucky!'

'Bit of a lame prediction, isn't it?' Sara observed as she took her place next to Memphis.

'Not to a Big Chunx fan like me,' said Fido Tennant from the desk in front. '*I'm* going to grab one at break time.'

'Because you believe the sock?'

He smiled. 'Because I believe in scoffing chocolate bars at least three times a day.'

Just then, Michelle Harris burst in. 'Ginger, Big Stitch was right!' she cried. 'Thomas Doughty had some bad luck. He's hurt his ankle—the prediction came true!'

Sara frowned. 'Another big tick for Big Stitch?'

'It's true!' Ashley Lamb appeared behind Michelle, red-faced from rushing. 'Thomas fell in the cloakrooms, and there was this big full moon stitched on one of the bags!'

The class erupted in excited chattering.

 31

Vicki gasped louder than anyone. 'That's amazing! How did you *know*, Ginger?'

She shrugged. 'Big Stitch just picks up the vibes.'

'Yeah, but *how*?'

Carefully, Ginger pulled the sock puppet from her hand. 'My gran says that there's a ley line running between my house and this school. You know, like an ancient pathway of prehistoric power.' She flourished her knitted partner. 'Big Stitch used to be just a regular sock—one of a pair knitted by an old gypsy friend of my gran's . . . '

Sara frowned. Under normal circumstances, admitting that you wore knitted gypsy socks would be committing social suicide. But the class was hanging on her every word.

'We must have walked that ley line together so many times,' said Ginger, 'that over the months, this sock *absorbed* its mystical energy.'

'Ugh,' said Fido. 'Didn't you ever wash it?'

Ginger didn't rise to his cheesy bait. 'When it started to wear out, I made it into a sock puppet—Big Stitch. From the moment I put him on, I *knew* . . . I knew he was special.'

Memphis grinned at Sara. 'A wise old sole?'

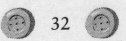

'Sounds kind of corny to me,' said Sara, forcing a smile back. It was easy to pour scorn on Ginger's unlikely story—but secretly she was more than a little creeped out by the news that the sock had been spot on once again.

'It was amazing,' said Ginger. 'It was like . . . *I* was the puppet and *he* was working *me*! He told me he was the Sock of Ages . . . That he had looked ahead and knew we would do great things together . . . ' She shrugged. 'And the rest is history.'

Therese frowned. 'Don't you mean the future?'

While the rest of the class groaned or rolled their eyes, Sara glanced across at Vicki Starling two desks away. She seemed lost in a world of her own, head in the clouds, eyes far away and dreamy.

Elise put a hand on Vicki's arm. 'You see, sweetie? The sock's never wrong!'

Denise placed a hand on her other arm. 'Yeah, you and Sam *must* be meant for each other! Maybe you just haven't seen the real him yet.'

Since both arms were taken, Therese placed her hand on Vicki's knee. 'Er . . . ' Clearly she

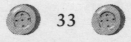

was struggling for her own pearl of wisdom. 'What they just said!'

'I hear what you're saying, guys,' said Vicki, with a sickly smile. 'But I don't know. Should I *really* give Sam a second chance? What if the real him is just as annoying and gross as the fake him?'

'Actually, she has a good point, there,' said Sara.

'Scary prospect,' Memphis agreed.

Just then, Sam walked in, helping Thomas walk to his desk. Knowing looks passed between the classmates. Ginger blinked through her big glasses, her expression unreadable.

'She warned you, Doughty,' called Ruth Cook. 'Shame you didn't listen. Tough bananas for Sports Day now, isn't it?'

Thomas shot her a dirty look.

'Have you seen the school nurse?' Sara called.

He shook his head. 'I don't believe in nurses. I already *know* I'm not going to be able to take part.'

'That's really sad, Thomas,' said Fido, as if he was so, so sorry. But when he turned round in his seat again to face Sara and Memphis, he wore

34

a jaunty grin. 'I didn't stand a chance of winning the hurdles with Thomas running,' he hissed. 'Now things are looking up!'

Clearly Vicki felt the same way. 'Hey, guys! Sam helped Thomas get to class with his bad ankle! Isn't that sweet!'

'Sweet?' echoed Sara. 'Dragging the poor guy all the way to Killer's geography class? That's more like adding insult to injury!'

Vicki gave her a *What would you know about it?* look.

Before Sara could respond with a telling look of her own, Killer Collier creaked into the classroom. Everyone fell silent. He was short, squat, and ancient, with a face like a month-old apple that had grown a white, whiskery moustache. He only ever wore one suit, a starched navy blue pinstripe number that was probably all the rage in 1942. Oddly, although it *looked* clean enough, little clouds of dust seemed to gust from it with every step.

But while he looked frail, Killer Collier was actually as tough as the ancient leather uppers on his wrinkly feet. He had a temper that could reduce fellow teachers to tears, never mind his pupils.

'Textbooks open at page seventy-six, please,' he wheezed. 'We'll be continuing our work on coastal erosion by exploring the phenomenon of longshore drift.'

'Whoopee,' sighed Memphis.

'Ball, that's enough backchat!' snapped Killer. 'Now, who can tell me where we got to last lesson?' He squinted around at his class. 'Mutton?'

Ginger jumped. 'Er . . . Let me think, it was something about ox-bow lakes—no, that's not it. Stacks? No . . . '

Unbelievably, still more wrinkles were appearing on Killer's face as his frown deepened dangerously. 'Come on, girl.'

Still Ginger kept on racking her brains. 'Um, we looked at those windbreak things they build on beaches to stop the sand washing away, didn't we? Or was that the week before?'

'She may be hot on the future but she's hopeless with the past!' hissed Memphis.

Sara nodded. Ginger seemed naturally scatty and her memory was pretty bad. Maybe that was why she felt happier talking about stuff that hadn't happened yet.

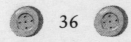 36

'Got it!' said Ginger. 'It was something about sand in water crashing against the rocks . . .'

Killer Collier could stand no more. 'Attrition!' he exploded.

'Bless you,' said Sam.

It was the sort of wisecrack Sam just couldn't resist, and the class fell about with laughter. But Killer's face had turned tomato red, and he marched stiffly up to Sam's desk.

'Innocent!' he screamed, and the laughter stopped dead.

Killer wasn't part of the 'soft-but-scary voice' brigade of teachers, like Horrible Hayes the history teacher. He was one of the loud, shout-in-your-face ones, who sprayed you with spit while they scared you to death.

'You are here for a single period only,' Killer yelled. 'If you choose to waste a single further second of my time I shall waste yours—at lunchtime each and every day this week.'

'Sorry, sir,' said Sam sheepishly.

'And you, Mutton, will join him,' roared Killer Collier, 'since you seem to pay so little attention to my lessons. And while we're at it, so will the

 37

rest of you, for laughing like that—if I hear one more word!'

Sara gulped. The whole class sat frozen with fear.

'So, longshore drift . . . ' Killer said more calmly, shuffling back to his desk where a pile of exercise books sat teetering. 'While Miss Mutton tries to remember where we got up to last time you, Sam Innocent, will hand out the workbooks. Last week's homework has been marked.' He glowered round the room. 'And my goodness me, what a painful task *that* was.'

Sam got up and took the pile, tiptoeing round the room and placing them on people's desks with exaggerated care and quietness. He spent several seconds placing Sara's in front of her as if it was made of crystal, and she gave him a warning look. He just smiled. Some people settled for pushing their luck, but Sara had soon learned that Sam preferred to rugby tackle his, truss it up and heave it over the edge of a cliff to go splat a mile below.

She checked her book. The set essay had been on the negative effects of tourism on coastal towns. She'd got a B. Not bad.

But what about Fido? He was drumming his fingers quietly on the desk, waiting for his book. Would the sock be right again?

Ginger was looking meek and timid after her telling off, accepting her book from Sam without comment. Vicki Starling gave him a dazzling smile as he approached to hand over her book. Blushing bright red, Sam tossed the book carelessly in front of her and walked straight on to Fido.

Sara, like the rest of the class, watched closely as he opened his book . . .

And gave a squawk of alarm.

'Do you have a problem, Tennant?' rasped Killer, giving him the evil eye.

'No, sir,' said Fido stiffly.

'Then, keep quiet, boy!'

Fido shut up, but he angled the book so that Sara could see over his shoulder. There, in Killer's familiar scrawl, was a single line of red-pen comments:

The wurst work it has been my missfortune to mark in years.

E-

'An E minus for Fido,' muttered Memphis. 'But an A plus for the sock!'

'It's Killer who deserves an E minus,' whispered Sara. 'For his terrible spelling!'

BREAKTIME

The rest of the lesson dragged by as slowly as a pebble travelling from one end of the beach to the other—only quieter. Sam sighed as he counted off the lesson's last seconds. Longshore drift? It *shore* hadn't taken him long to drift off . . .

Finally the hooter sounded for break and people dared to speak again—mainly mutters of disbelief that they had survived such a dull lesson without their heads exploding. But once Killer Collier had shuffled out of the room ready to terrorize his next class, a new subject for discussion presented itself.

'E minus!' groaned Fido. 'I thought I'd done all right on that homework!'

'Ha!' Ruth Cook laughed at him. 'Even *I* only got a D!'

'It's just like Big Stitch said!' gasped Therese. 'He's right *again*!'

 41

Sam frowned. This was getting kind of spooky. Big Stitch's success rate—like the old sock itself—was not to be sniffed at. And you didn't have to be Einstein to work out that the more predictions the sock got right, the more convinced Vicki would be that she and Sam were meant for each other—however hard he tried to put her off. He closed his eyes wearily and, when he opened them again, saw that Vicki was looking at him with a lovelorn expression. Sam quickly pulled a funny face at her and looked the other way.

He heard a gaggle of giggles as she and her clone club walked past him on their way out.

'*Au revoir*, Sam,' called Vicki. 'I'll be seeing you soon, OK?'

'You'll have to look hard,' muttered Sam, not looking up. He had preferred it when she used to blank him, not caring he was even alive—at least that had been an honest reaction.

Fido was expressing his own honest reaction to Killer's low grade in a variety of four-letter words. It was weird about Fido, Sam decided. He was naturally brainy and didn't have to work too hard at getting good grades. Sam, on the other hand, was more crafty than bright, and yet he'd managed a B; more than he had expected, especially after the dumb bit he'd written about kids in seaside towns being traumatized by the rising prices of ice creams.

'Killer's gone ga-ga,' grumbled Fido. 'Silly old duffer should have retired fifty years ago.'

'Maybe you should complain,' said Sara.

'Complain? To Killer Collier?' Fido shook his head. 'Not likely.'

'You should! He can't have been concentrating properly,' Sara argued. 'He spelt stuff wrong!'

'Maybe they spelt them that way in Victorian times when he was growing up,' Sam suggested.

'Whatever,' sighed Fido. 'I guess I'll just have to put it down to bad luck.'

'No such thing as luck,' said Doubting Thomas. He glared over at Ginger. 'And there's no such thing as fortune telling socks!'

Ginger walked quickly from the room. But Sam noticed she looked a little bit rattled. Why, when public belief in her stupid sock had never been stronger?

'I'm going to cheer myself up with a Big Chunx bar,' Fido announced. 'Got to keep my energy levels up for this afternoon.'

 43

'Sounds like a good idea,' said Sam. 'The chocolate bit, I mean. I'll come with you.'

'Better be quick, boys,' Sara warned them. 'According to the sock, they're going to run out any minute!'

'Wish *I* could,' said Doubting Thomas, as he hobbled out of the room, pulling some coins from his pocket. 'See you later.'

'Yeah, see ya, mate.' Sam watched him go. 'Shame about Thomas,' he remarked.

'Yeah, it's really rough,' said Fido.

They looked at each other.

Sam grinned. 'Let's beat him to the snack bar.'

'Cool,' said Fido. 'That's one less person we'll have to fight for the last bar!'

The two of them sprinted from the classroom.

Sara watched them go with a smile. 'Looks like Vicki's got herself a real knight in shining armour there!'

'I'll bet she's not used to guys playing hard to get,' said Memphis, leading the way outside. 'It'll probably make her even keener!'

'Sam's a marked man, all right,' Sara agreed. 'That Ginger Mutton has a lot to answer for.'

'Speaking of marked men—gotta feel sorry for Thomas. Big Stitch has made more predictions about him than anyone else!'

'I wonder why?' mused Sara. 'It's not like he even believes in that stuff.'

'Maybe that's it,' said Memphis. 'The sock is teaching him a lesson . . . '

But as they passed the cloaks on their way to the playground, it seemed that someone was trying to teach *Ginger* a lesson—Carl Witlow. He was standing over her menacingly, while she looked wide-eyed and worried up at him.

'History repeating,' muttered Sara, signalling Memphis to wait a moment. 'Everything OK, Ginger?'

'Oh, er . . . yes, I'm fine,' she said timidly, hands behind her back as if she was hiding something there.

Carl Witlow turned to Sara with an ugly look on his face. 'Push off and drop dead,' he snarled. 'We're having a little chat.'

'Yeah, well, I doubt you know enough long words for a *big* chat,' said Sara. 'Speaking of

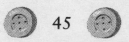

45

size—why don't you pick on someone who's your own?'

Carl gave her a crooked smile. 'What, like your baldy mate there?'

Memphis took a step closer to Sara and crossed her arms. 'Just try it, bog-breath.'

'Thanks, but I . . . I can handle things here,' said Ginger bravely, her voice trembling along with her skinny legs.

'Haven't you got the message yet, Witlow?' Sara demanded. Her heart was racing, but she wasn't about to let this bully know she was scared. 'If you truly believe in that sock, well, it's your problem. But it can't answer questions, it can only—'

'Who are you to tell me what that stupid sock of hers can or can't do?' he hissed, barging past her and Memphis. 'Get in my way again and you'll be sorry!'

Sara felt a wave of relief swash over her. 'Thanks for backing me up, Memph.'

'Didn't have much choice, did I?' said Memphis wryly. 'You're such a do-gooder.'

'I'm not. I just hate bullies. You OK, Ginger?'

'I'm fine. I'm perfect, really.' Ginger had

turned and crouched over her bag. Sara saw she was fondling the fabric of her sock with both hands, as if it was some kind of miniature security blanket. She sounded close to tears. 'Please, just leave me alone. You'll only make things worse.'

Sarah frowned. 'Is that sweat-ape picking on you or something?'

'Look, take a ride and move aside, OK?' said Ginger, trying to act cool but barely making lukewarm. 'I'm waiting to meet my mate Cass, so why don't you just get out of here.'

'Cass?' Memphis raised an eyebrow. 'That would be Cassie Shaw, right?'

'Right. Cass.'

'The hottest girl in year ten is your best pal?'

Ginger scowled. 'Well, what's so funny about that?'

'I'm not laughing,' said Sara.

'Look, I don't need you judging me, OK? I'm not asking you to believe in Big Stitch—'

'It's the idea of you and Cassie Shaw buddying up I find harder to swallow,' said Memphis, and Sara nudged her in the ribs.

'Get lost!' said Ginger crossly. 'Why don't

 47

you go and poke your nose in someone else's business?'

'Huh!' said Memphis. 'That's rich—you and your sock poke your noses in other people's business before it even happens!'

'Big Stitch doesn't have a nose! He has a toe!' retorted Ginger hotly. 'We can't help it if we can tell the future. It's a gift! And *I* can't help it if cool people want to hang with me, can I?'

'Oh, come on, Memphis,' said Sara. She acted as if she wasn't bothered, but couldn't help feeling a tiny bit hurt by Ginger's reaction. 'We're obviously not cool enough for her. Let's leave her to it, if that's what she really wants.'

Tossing her head, she walked away with Memphis.

'That girl's got a real attitude problem,' Memphis grumped.

Sara smoothed her blonde hair out over her shoulders. 'You *were* a bit mean to her, Memph.'

'Well, she was a bit mean to you.' Memphis came to a sudden stop at the edge of the cloaks as a good-looking girl with long black locks and a nose like a ski-slope slinked past in the opposite direction. 'Hey, and there's her bestest mate,

"Cass" Shaw, come to keep their date! C'mon, let's loiter.'

'Memphis,' Sara complained, but her gawky friend was already creeping closer, moving aside a couple of sports bags so she could look in on the unlikely rendezvous. Against her better judgement, Sara followed.

'Hey, Ginge,' said Cassie.

'Cass!' cried Ginger, straightening her chunky glasses and giving her a big ditzy smile. 'It's like, totally amazing to see you. How are you—?'

'I'm great, thanks,' said Cassie. 'So, has Big Stitch had anything more to say about me?'

'Uh . . . nothing lately.'

'What, nothing at all?' Cassie pouted. 'He does know who I am, right?'

'Everyone knows who *you* are, Cass,' said Ginger, as if she was speaking to royalty or something. 'So, shall we go chill with your friends?'

Cass smiled and shook her head. 'You know, they're kind of busy right now,' she said. 'But we might be able to slot you in at the end of lunch break? You'll have to do your thing with the sock for us, of course—it's *so* funny. I'll send someone here to pick you up.'

 49

'When?'

'I don't know exactly—just hang around, 'K?
See you!'

'Sure, thanks, Cass,' said Ginger, and Sara's heart
went out to her as she tried to handle her disap-
pointment. 'I . . . I'll maybe see you later, then.'

'Maybe,' she agreed brightly. 'Ciao!'

Cassie tossed her hair, gave a little wave and
strutted off.

'So much for Ginger's best buddy,' said
Memphis quietly.

Sara nodded. 'No entry to the A-list without
a sock—when it suits *them*.'

Ginger waited a few moments till she thought
she was alone, then burst into tears. She ran out
of the cloaks and into the girls' toilets.

'Should we see if she's all right?' Sara
suggested.

'I think we should do as she told us to,' sighed
Memphis, heading for the playground. 'Mind our
own business.'

'Tell me to mind my own business if you like,'
said Fido as he and Sam made tracks for the

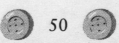

snack bar, 'but how come you're acting like Vicki Starling's a pig in knickers?'

'I'm not. She's hot,' Sam admitted. 'But I refuse to be set up by a sock. The whole thing is crazy.'

'That's what Thomas Doughty thought,' said Fido.

'Don't tell me you actually believe in Big Stitch?'

'Well, he was right about my homework. He's been right about a lot of things.'

'*He?*' Sam felt like pulling out his hair. '*It* is a *sock*!'

Fido shrugged. 'Knitted by a gypsy, Ginger says.'

'Well, she's not going to admit it's from Tesco, is she?'

'Even so,' said Fido. 'If I was given a chance with Vicki Starling, I reckon I'd take it.'

But as they turned the corner, the conversation was forgotten. A massive crowd had gathered around the snack bar counter. People were jostling and shoving each other about.

A woman's voice rang out from the serving hatch—it was Mrs Hurst the Games teacher, who manned (or womanned) the snack bar at break times. 'Get in line!' she shouted. 'I'm not serving anyone unless there's some order here!'

'Bundle!' somebody shouted behind them, and Sam and Fido suddenly found themselves being swept into the heart of the scrum. An elbow was shoved in Sam's face and someone trod on his foot. He pushed back at whoever was pushing him.

'What's going on?' gasped Sam.

'There's a rush on for Big Chunx bars, stupid,' said a wiry kid ahead of him. 'There's a rumour going around that they're going to run out.'

Fido tried to speak through a mouthful of someone's arm. 'There are other chocolate bars, aren't there? Why all the fuss?'

'Because they're half price, stupid,' said a girl as she pushed past him, clawing her way through the dense bundle of bodies. 'Special promotion. Didn't you see the sign as you came in?'

'All I saw was this guy's butt as I was shoved into it,' Sam retorted as the girl jostled him out of the way. 'Hey, get in line!'

'Get over yourself,' said the girl. 'There's cheap chocolate at stake!'

'All right, that's enough!' came a bellowing

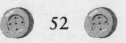

voice from the back of the scrum. Almost every-one jumped in the air with the shock wave. Penter had entered, and he didn't look pleased. His red eyes were narrowed and you could almost see his spiky beard bristling with ire. 'Let's have an orderly queue, you reprobates. Now!'

Like a snake uncoiling, the bundle of people slowly resolved itself into a single line. Fido and Sam found themselves jostled further and further back until the snack bar itself was lost from view.

'Thank you, Mr Penter,' said Mrs Hurst. 'But I think I can manage from here.'

'Of course, Mrs Hurst,' said Penter, loping off again. 'But just behave yourselves, *children*—or I'll put every single one of you on detention.'

'This isn't fair,' groaned Sam. 'We'll be here all break, now.'

'Big Chunx are sold out!' shouted Mrs Hurst. 'No more Big Chunx.'

'You're kidding!' Sam slapped his forehead in disbelief.

'That's what Big Stitch predicted!' said Fido, frowning. 'Before Geography.'

'But how did Ginger *know*?' cried Sam. 'How?'

A ragged shout went up from people in the

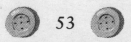

queue. 'The sock was right!' 'Big Stitch said this would happen!' 'Praise the sock!'

'I can't stand it.' Sam clenched his fists. 'My stomach was set on a Big Chunx, and that stupid scrappy sock has messed things up *again* . . . '

A pointy-headed boy with a quiff turned to Sam with a confidential air. 'Big Stitch is hardly scrappy, you know. *I* hear he was sewn with golden hair plucked from the sacred yak of the orient.'

'Stop *yakking* about that stupid Big Stitch!' shouted Sam, loud enough to send the boy staggering backwards in alarm. 'I'm sick and tired of this dumb sock and its stupid predictions!'

The entire queue fell silent at his outburst.

'This sock is a public menace!' Sam yelled as Fido took a few discreet steps away from him. 'It's getting out of control! Someone needs to sew its gob shut! Someone needs to dip the thing in bleach! Someone needs to get some scissors and . . . '

He trailed off, suddenly aware that everyone was looking at him as if he was nuts.

'How about we get some fresh air, Sam?' said Fido, grabbing him by the sleeve and dragging him out through the cafeteria doors.

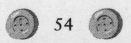

'No, wait a minute,' said Sam, pulling free of Fido's grip. He was hungry and still mad, and needed to sound off about it. 'We have to do something. Big Stitch is really a Big Stitch-*up*— it's the only explanation that makes sense.'

Fido blinked. 'What are you on about?'

'I mean that the only way that Ginger could predict these things is if she knows in advance that they're going to happen! Like, maybe she knows someone in the snack bar who told her Big Chunx would be on special offer today.'

'Maybe,' said Fido doubtfully. 'But what about all the other stuff, like Thomas slipping on soap, and my geography homework?'

'Ginger could have an accomplice. Someone whose job is to help her seem more convincing.'

'Oh, come off it! Who could be bothered to do that?'

'I don't know.' Sam looked at Fido meaningfully. 'But *you* were trying to persuade me to go out with Vicki Starling before, weren't you?'

'Just trying to make you see what you were missing,' said Fido, puzzled.

'If I did, the prediction would come true, wouldn't it?' said Sam. 'And just suppose you handed in homework to Killer Collier that you *knew* was bad. You could tip Ginger off and she could make a good prediction out of it!'

'Oh, yeah?' Fido glared at him. 'And I suppose I dropped that bar of soap for Thomas to slip on too, did I?'

'You could have!' Sam challenged. 'How would I know?'

'What would I get out of doing something like that?' said Fido furiously. 'Why would I want to make Ginger look good?'

'I don't know, you tell me!' said Sam. 'But there's got to be some explanation for that sock's success rate, hasn't there?'

'You're sick, Innocent,' said Fido. And he turned around and stalked off without another word.

Sam watched him go, and suddenly felt like dirt. 'I am *sick*,' he sighed. 'Sick of that sock!'

Sounding off at his friends wasn't going to help him get to the bottom of the mystery of the Big Stitch-Up. He had to expose whatever scam Ginger was running. He would need to take a more subtle approach.

It had to be a scam . . . didn't it?

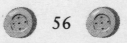

Sam set off for a long, hungry walk on his own, lost in his thoughts.

Sara and Memphis had spent a fairly average break chatting in the playground. Before the hooter went for the start of the next lesson, Sara decided to pay a visit to the girls' loos.

But when she got inside, she heard sobbing coming from one of the cubicles, and another girl's voice. Sara told herself not to be nosy and took the cubicle two doors down. But she couldn't help but overhear the sniff-ridden conversation.

Ginger Mutton was the girl who was crying. Obviously she'd gone in here after Cassie Shaw's visit and hadn't come out again.

'I never see you any more, Ginge,' said the other girl. 'We used to be best friends. Am I not good enough for you now or something, is that it? I mean, I may not be Cassie Shaw, but—'

'It's not that, Mindy,' said Ginger. 'It's just that Big Stitch has opened up so many doors for me.'

'If you keep on doing what you're doing,' said Mindy, 'you're going to get into trouble. *Big* trouble.'

'I'm not stopping now,' said Ginger, backing up her words with a staggering sniff. 'I can't go back to being a nobody again.'

'Gee, thanks.'

'I'm going to see this thing through. No matter what.'

'You're crazy! This *thing*, as you call it, is . . .'

Yes? thought Sara, on the edge of her toilet seat. What *is this thing, as you call it?* But just then, Ginger or Mindy flushed and the rest of the conversation was lost in a gurgling, rushing roar of toilet water.

Hardly sounds flushed with success, thought Sara.

She quickly finished and opened the cubicle door. But Ginger and Mindy had already gone.

Periods Three and Four
Double History

Sam got to Horrible Hayes's history room ahead of the end-of-break hooter and the rest of the class. He didn't want to run into Fido—he knew he'd been wrong to accuse him but he was still too sore to be sorry. And he certainly didn't want to run into Vicki and her cronies again. Once news of the Big Chunx incident spread, Ginger's sock would be more revered than ever.

Speak of the devil—or at the least, one of his little helpers—here was Ginger now. Her eyes were red and blotchy as if she'd been crying. She was careful not to look at him, as if she was scared of what he might say.

Very wise, thought Sam. Truthfully, he wanted to come on all tough with her; to interrogate her mercilessly and learn the truth about whatever stunt she was trying to pull. But Ginger looked so miserable he couldn't bring himself to say a single word to her in case she burst into tears.

Ginger put her bag on the desk and started rummaging through it. Slowly at first; then more and more desperately.

Michelle Harris was the next person in. 'Wow, Ginger, you and Big Stitch were right about the Big Chunx bars running out!' she said admiringly. 'That was totally—'

'Oh my God!' cried Ginger, her ransacked bag slipping off the desk and *BANG!* to the floor. 'Big Stitch—he's gone!'

Michelle stared. 'Gone?'

Sam turned around and frowned. Could it be true?

Ginger nodded, white faced. 'Look!' She held up a shiny black button. 'I left him in my bag at break. His eye snagged on my zipper—but that's all that's left. He's been . . . *socknapped*!'

'You what?' said Ashley, waddling into the room.

'Big Stitch has been stolen!' squeaked Michelle.

'Never!' he said, scandalized.

'All that's left is an eye!' she said fearfully.

'How come he never saw *that* coming?' asked Sam innocently. 'With his other eye, I mean?'

'Who would do such a thing?' Ginger bemoaned.

'Sam Innocent might.'

Sam looked up to find Fido standing in the doorway.

'Come off it, mate,' said Sam.

He shrugged. 'We all heard you threatening the sock by the snack bar.'

'That's true, you did,' said Ashley. 'I was there.'

'Sam threatened a sock?' That was Sara, coming up behind Fido. 'When?'

'He stole Big Stitch!' wailed Ginger.

'I never!' said Sam fiercely.

'I believe him,' said Vicki Starling, forcing her way through Sara and Fido. 'Sam just wouldn't do something like that.'

'I might,' Sam argued. 'But I didn't.'

'We've only got your word for that,' said Fido, stirring things up.

'You're not convincing anyone, Fido,' said Sam, though he could feel himself turning red. 'This might be a double bluff. If you're working with Ginger she probably *told* you to steal the sock.'

'What?' cried Memphis, who'd come in on the whole conversation a bit late. 'Fido and Ginger are working together?'

'We're not!' shouted Fido. 'I've had enough of your accusations, Innocent.'

'Well, I've had enough of yours!'

'I've hardly started!'

'What's got into you two?' asked Sara, standing between them. 'Calm down, both of you!'

'No,' cried Vicki excitedly, 'they should fight if they want to!' She looked up at Sam admiringly. 'Sam will flatten him, won't you!'

Sara frowned. 'Stay out of this.'

'Who's going to make me?' asked Vicki, standing up and folding her arms.

'*I* will,' said Sam. 'Just shut up a minute.'

'Sam,' gasped Vicki, clearly shocked, 'don't talk to *me* like that!'

'Too fast for you was it?' asked Memphis.

Sara threw her arms up. 'And don't you start!'

'What's going on?' demanded Ruthless Cook, swaggering into the room.

'Big Stitch has been stolen!' cried Michelle.

'And Sam's accused me of setting up Ginger's prophecies to make them come true,' said Fido angrily.

Ruthless shook her head. 'You're mental, Innocent.'

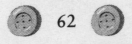

'Yeah, how could Fido possibly do that?' scoffed Elise, walking in with Denise and Therese.

'And even if I *could*, why should I want to give myself an E minus?' Fido argued.

'I only said you *might* have done,' Sam protested.

'And how did I make Thomas Doughty slip on the soap, or Cassie Shaw fall for John Pidgin?'

'I don't know,' Sam conceded. 'Look, I take it all back, OK? I went off into one, and I'm sorry. I didn't know what I was saying!'

'No. You didn't.' Fido half-smiled. 'But I guess you can't help being stupid.'

'True,' grinned Sam.

Ashley tutted like a man in the know. 'Reckon you knew what you were saying when you threatened Big Stitch.'

Sam sighed. 'Now look what you've started, Fido!'

'Well, *you* started it really,' Fido pointed out, 'back in the snack bar.'

'Look, Fido, I *told* you I was sorry about that—'

'Don't start fighting again,' said Sara, coming between them.

 63

'Sam, tell *me* you're sorry for shouting,' said Vicki.

'Oh, get over it,' groaned Memphis.

'I'm *not* sorry for shouting,' said Sam, 'I enjoy shouting!'

'Did he shout at you, sweetie?' cooed Elise.

'He didn't mean it,' Denise assured her.

'What didn't he mean?' asked Therese, confused.

'Everyone be quiet and listen!'

The class fell silent as Big Stitch's distinctive squawk rang out around the room. Ginger had gone curiously quiet, and now Sam understood why.

Sitting cross-legged on her desk, she'd slipped off both shoes. Her left foot was sockless—because she was wearing the sock on her hand. It looked a bit sweaty and bedraggled, and Big Stitch's single eye was clumsily sticky-taped to the fabric around her knuckles so it actually looked more like a glistening nose.

'What is *that* thing?' spluttered Sam.

'The spirit of Big Stitch is restless,' Ginger intoned, throwing her voice with eerie effectiveness. 'He will hop through the long, dark night of the sole until the wicked sock-rustler who holds him now is brought to justice. But mean-while, he still has some prophecies to make.'

'How can it?' said Sara, frowning. 'It's been nicked!'

'I still have his eye,' said Ginger in her normal voice. 'This button may bind him to a second sock.'

'My name is Little Knit,' said the puny piece of footwear.

'How about that?' said Sam. 'A little nit with a Little Knit!'

But the rest of the class shushed him.

'Horrible Hayes will be here any minute,' said Vicki. 'I want to hear what Little Knit has to say.'

'Hey, Ginge, don't you have to say the rhyme of time or whatever to get him speaking?' Memphis enquired.

Ginger looked at her, lost for a moment. Then she seemed to recover, nodded, and spoke quickly to Little Knit:

> 'Substitute sock
> Against the clock
> Speak to your flock—
> And try not to shock!'

'You silly old crock,' muttered Sam.

'I have a prophecy for Sara Knot,' the sock pretender announced.

'Wow!' Fido clapped a hand on Sara's arm. 'From Knit to Knot!'

Sam cracked up, and he and Fido high-fived; grievances forgotten and friends again through the healing power of weak puns.

'Shut up, you two,' Sara complained. 'Go on then, Ginger.'

'I . . . er . . . ' Ginger seemed distracted, her eyes scrunched up with concentration as the sock spoke slowly. 'If you go to the . . . No, that's not it. If you, um . . . hold on, wait for it . . . '

'It's you two,' said Elise crossly. 'You've put her off!'

'It takes time to build up a relationship with a new sock,' Ginger explained. 'Wait . . . erm . . . '

Little Knit reared up like a straggly snake. 'Sara Knot, if you stand outside the sports hall at breather you will have some good luck.'

'Oh yeah?' Sara looked doubtful.

'Better watch out!' announced Doubting Thomas, who was just hobbling in through the door. 'Hayes is coming!'

Ashley went to the door to see. 'He is too! He'll confiscate Little Knit as soon as look at it!'

'Message for Vicki Starling,' squeaked Little Knit quickly.

'For me!' cried Vicki.

'As if,' snorted Doubting Thomas.

'Your true love . . . '

Vicki's hands flew to her mouth. 'Sam?'

Little Knit paused, tantalizingly, before concluding: 'He is not what he seems.'

'He is!' said Ruthless Cook unexpectedly.

Sam blinked. 'I am?'

'He seems to be a prat and he is one!' she laughed.

'Totally lame,' said Sam.

Memphis shook her head. 'No, that's Thomas after his fall.'

'And Samuel Innocent!' croaked the sock menacingly.

Therese gasped. 'Sam?'

'The prat,' added Ruth helpfully.

'I have a warning for you!'

'So have I!' hissed Ashley from the doorway. 'Hayes is ten seconds away from coming in!'

'I am sorry to say you are in for a spell of bad

fortune,' said the sock. 'By the end of the day you will be left black and blue!'

Sam stared. 'So now I'm being threatened by a *sock*?'

'Here comes Hayes!' squealed Ashley, dashing away from the door. 'Quick!'

Everyone dived back to their places. While Sara and Memphis skidded to their seats at the back of the class, Sam swung himself into a chair beside Thomas Doughty at the front. Ginger jumped off her desk at the far side of the classroom, struggling desperately to yank the sock from her wrist. It seemed stuck.

At the desk to Sam's right, Elise and Vicki were watching Ginger in horror. 'She'll never get it off in time!'

A long, agonizing second passed.

But when Horrible Hayes entered a moment later, the class was seated quietly and expectantly. All except Ginger Mutton, who seemed to be blowing her nose noisily on a very long soggy white tissue.

She's craftier than she looks, Sam noted.

Hayes's flint-grey eyes twitched behind his gold-rimmed spectacles, and he stroked his black,

satanic beard. 'You're all far too quiet,' he observed. 'What's been going on?'

'Nothing, sir,' said Sam brightly. 'Just waiting around, keen to learn.'

Hayes gave him a dark look. But Ginger distracted him with another long blow on her woolly tissue.

Hayes looked crossly over at Ginger. 'Miss Mutton, will you stop that revolting noise?'

'Yes, sir,' she mumbled, as she finally tore her hand free of the sock and shoved it in her pocket.

'Now, then,' said Hayes. 'Continuing our very interesting look at famous figures of the sixteenth century, today we'll be studying Michel de Notredame—the man, the myth.'

'With a name like Michelle I'm not surprised he wath taken for a mith,' joked Sam quietly.

'I believe you heard me perfectly, Mr Innocent.' Hayes bore down on him. 'Now, by what name is he *better* known?'

'Gloria?'

Hayes's eyes narrowed to black slits, and the few classmates brave enough to titter soon shut up. 'He is known as *Nostradamus*,' said Hayes. 'And unless you want a detention every day till

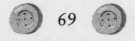 69

you die, you'll stop your tedious clowning and tell me what he was famous for!'

Sam glanced over at Ginger Mutton. 'Telling the future, sir.'

'Correct. Although, in his *own* time, he was a very famous doctor,' said Hayes, warming to his subject and striding off to his desk. 'His reputation was ruined when his family died of the plague, despite his efforts to save them. He didn't make a single prediction until he was almost fifty years old . . . '

Sam heard a quiet dragging sound. He looked down to see his bag inching its way away from him across the floor. Elise was pulling on the strap!

He frowned. 'What are you doing?' he mouthed at her, as she hauled his bag out of reach and under her desk.

But it was Vicki, beside her, who answered. 'Checking you're not the socknapper!' she mouthed back.

'Little Knit said you're not what you seem,' added Elise.

'Neither's that sock!' Sam whispered furiously.

Hayes fixed Sam with his armour-piercing eyes. 'If you've quite finished, Mr Innocent?'

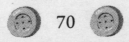

He glared at Elise. 'Sorry, sir.'

'Talk of Nostradamus's powers swept through the country,' Hayes went on. 'And when Queen Catherine de Medici started to believe in his predictions, his popularity grew even greater . . . '

History repeating! thought Sam. *Cassie Shaw believing in Ginger has made her a school celeb!*

Slowly, quietly, Elise was unzipping his bag until it gaped open.

'But Nostradamus had powerful enemies as well as friends,' said Hayes. 'The Justices of Paris were looking into his so-called unnatural practices . . . '

While Hayes moaned on, Elise and Vicki were discreetly rifling through Sam's bag under the desk. He fumed as they screwed up their noses. Of course, he'd never taken out last week's muddy PE kit or that old half-eaten sandwich . . .

How dare these girls go through his stuff!

He flailed out a leg, trying to hook his bag strap with his foot. But Elise gently nudged the strap away. He lunged again, stretching out even further—and the chair slipped from under him.

Sam landed on his butt and the class erupted into laughter.

'Innocent, I have had more than enough of you!' bellowed Hayes. 'Outside. Now!'

Dazed on the floor, for a moment Sam thought his teacher was challenging him to a fight. 'Sir?'

'Get out, boy! Stand outside the door and I'll deal with you later!'

Sam nodded sheepishly. He noticed Vicki and Elise looking guiltily down at their desks, and he noticed Sara too, giving him that half-amused, half-despairing look of hers.

And he noticed Ginger, too. The look she gave him was shifty and strange, sad but resigned. A kind of helpless, *'it's out of my hands'* type of look.

The lesson dragged on. Hayes wrote out translations for some of Nostradamus's prophecies on the chalkboard, and split the class into groups. Each group tackled a different translation to try and work out what it might mean. Sara and Memphis were teamed up with—predictably— Vicki, Elise, and Therese.

'How can I concentrate on ancient history,' sighed Vicki. 'I am, like, so totally confused! Is Sam a good guy, or a goodbye?'

 72

'At least there's no proof he's the socknapper,' Elise reminded her. 'No sign of Big Stitch in Sam's bag. Only freaky gross boy stuff.'

'Don't remind me.' Vicki shuddered. 'I mean, did you check that mouldy sandwich? *Hello?*'

'Well, Sock Junior did say that Sam wasn't what he seemed,' said Sara with a tight smile. 'Maybe he's addicted to going through the garbage when no one's looking.'

'Do you think so?' said Therese, wide-eyed.

'She's joking,' said Elise. 'And she's *so* not funny.'

'She's just jealous,' said Vicki.

'As if!' snorted Sara.

Elise nodded. 'Everyone knows she's crazy about Sam.'

'I am not!'

'Correct,' said Memphis. '*Sara* Knot. Could we change the subject, ladies? I've had a bellyful of this sock rubbish today.'

Sara smiled. 'Hey, d'you think Nostradamus had help from a sock?'

Memphis grinned. '*Mais oui!*'

'May we what?' asked Therese, confused and frustrated. 'I don't get it!'

 73

'Don't get what?' boomed Hayes.

'Er, this line here,' said Memphis quickly. '"In the very near year, not far from Venus." What is *that* supposed to mean?'

'Almost all of Nostradamus's prophecies are vague and waffly,' said Hayes. 'This made it harder for people to prove him wrong, and allowed his followers to twist his prophecies' meanings to suit themselves. For instance . . . '

Sara soon drifted off. It was clear to her that any idiot could predict the future—the tricky part was getting it right. On the one hand, the likes of Nostradamus buried the meanings of their predictions in obscure verses. On the other hand—the small, freckled hand that wore a sock puppet—Big Stitch's predictions were incredibly precise, and yet right just about every time. So how *did* Ginger manage it?

'Are you going to hang around outside the sports hall at breather like the little nit says?' asked Memphis, once Hayes had gone off to hassle another group.

'I guess. I'm kind of curious.' Sara smiled. 'And who could turn down the chance of a little good luck? Especially after losing my bracelet.'

 74

'Let's hope some luck rubs off on Sam,' said Memphis. 'He's not had such a hot day, has he?'

'Are you kidding?' said Vicki. 'He's found out he's my true love!'

'Uh-huh,' Memphis nodded. 'My point proven.'

'Bite me,' said Vicki. 'I just wish I knew what Ginger meant when she said he wasn't what he seemed. I mean, is she trying to put me off him or something?'

'Maybe it's for your own protection,' said Memphis. 'I mean, he is supposed to wind up black and blue today . . . '

'I wonder when it'll happen,' said Therese, biting her lip.

'And I don't even know if I should kiss him better afterwards or not,' sighed Vicki.

'Don't you think we should try and *prevent* whatever's supposed to happen to him?' said Sara. 'That way he won't end up black and blue and he won't *need* kissing.'

'You can't fight destiny,' said Elise with conviction.

Sara looked over at the classroom door. 'If I know Sam, he'll at least get a few punches in.'

'No, no, no, Miss Mutton,' said Hayes irritably

 75

from across the classroom. 'I told *your* group to study the *second* translation!'

'I told you so, Ginger!' Ashley complained. 'I just thought you *must* be right, you know, since . . . '

'Sorry, everyone,' said Ginger, her crimson cheeks clashing dreadfully with her carrot-coloured hair.

'She's so scatty, isn't she?' Memphis mused. 'And yet with Big Stitch she acts like she's *so* on the case.'

'We'd better get on working out this rubbish,' sighed Sara. 'Or Hayes will be on *our* case!'

Sam was leaning heavily against the classroom door, bored, bored, bored, when he noticed a furtive looking kid loitering by the door to a nearby storeroom. The boy was older than Sam, and had a badly bleached mullet, thick lips, and a big, bulbous nose. He clutched a small plastic bag in one hand. Casually, he opened the storeroom door, and slipped inside.

'What's he up to?' wondered Sam, and crept away to investigate.

The boy was fiddling with something on top of the storeroom door. As Sam appeared he stopped and gave a guarded look.

'Bunking off?' asked Sam cheerfully.

'Yeah,' smirked the other lad. 'What about you?'

'Chucked out by Hayes for messing around.'

'Excellent,' said the other boy approvingly. 'My name's Baz. Who are you?'

'Sam.'

'Sam who?'

'Innocent.'

'Till proved—?'

'—guilty. Yep, that's the old favourite,' Sam agreed.

'I've heard of you, Innocent,' said Baz, grinning. 'I reckon you might want to help me out here.'

Sam raised an eyebrow. 'Oh yeah? What are you up to?'

'Setting a trap!'

'What sort of a trap?'

'Can you keeps yours closed?'

Sam nodded.

Baz lowered his voice. 'I'm playing a brilliant

  77

practical joke on this dumb, irritating big-headed kid who really fancies himself. At breather, he's going to get what's coming to him.'

'Cool! Sounds like he deserves it.'

'Want to give me a hand?'

'Beats hanging around outside Hayes's door!'

It was a good trick, Sam decided. Baz had taken six pots of paint. He planned to balance them carefully on top of the storeroom door with their lids off, so that the slightest force would send them toppling. When the unlucky victim came along, Baz would shove him into the door, the paint pots would spill and—SPLAT—a nice gloopy mess all over the target.

Sam held the door steady while Baz scrambled up to get the paint pots in position. Then, carefully, they pulled the door until it was almost closed and the danger on top hidden from view.

Baz shook hands with Sam. 'Good job, mate. Thanks!'

'Imagine this guy's face when that lot tips onto him,' grinned Sam.

'Well, hang around at breather and you won't have to imagine,' said Baz. 'You'll see all the action!'

'Will do. Catch you later!'

With a last smirk, Baz sloped shiftily away to wherever he had come from.

Sam smiled to himself. So much for bad fortune coming his way. If that had been true, Hayes would have caught him red-handed helping Baz.

But just as he returned to his spot outside the door, it opened. Hayes stared at him bleakly, his grey eyes twitching. Sam often had that effect on teachers.

'You'll be aware, Mr Innocent, that school finishes early after Sports Day?'

'Yes, sir,' said Sam uneasily.

'For you, it does not. Instead you shall report here, where you will catch up on the work you have missed. I shall prepare a letter for you to give to your parents explaining why you had to stay behind.'

'Yes, sir,' Sam sighed.

Looked like Little Knit was a chip off the old sock. He'd been right. It really *wasn't* Sam's lucky day.

BREATHER

Sam had barely taken two steps back inside the classroom when the siren sounded for breather. Ginger Mutton was first to zoom out through the door, a little red-haired streak budging Sam aside.

'Sorry,' she said. 'But I have to see somebody—fast!'

'Yeah, a head doctor,' muttered Sam.

'See you later, Innocent,' said Hayes as he went out himself. 'And don't be late!'

'No, sir.' His bag was back by his desk, and zipped up again. As Sam approached, Vicki took one look at him and went into conference mode with her Chic Clique, whispering and gossiping.

'Didn't find what you were looking for, then?' Sam asked pointedly. 'A patch of paisley? A little woollen tongue?'

Elise, Denise, and Therese stood up protectively.

 80

'Sam,' said Elise, 'you have to understand that Vicki's feeling emotionally drained after what she's gone through today. She really can't talk to you right now.' As one, they rose from their seats and walked towards the door. 'She needs time.'

'Oh?' Sam said, brightening. 'Well, feel free to look me up in a year or two.'

Sara strolled up. 'Enjoy yourself out there?'

'Actually it was OK.' Sam gave his best mysterious smile. 'I stayed busy.'

'Oh yes?' said Memphis, joining them. 'Weren't burning Big Stitch, were you?'

'I'm not the socknapper!' Sam protested. 'I have better things to do with my time!'

'So who did take it?' wondered Sara. 'Carl Witlow?'

Memphis smiled. 'Got to be a more likely suspect than Cassie Shaw.'

'He's a kid in the year above,' Sara explained. 'We've seen him hassling Ginger twice today already. He's after a prediction and whatever Ginger's told him, he doesn't buy it.'

'Well, I'm sure Little Knit will point a toe at the culprit before long,' said Sam. 'But never mind the sock-talk. Hang with me outside that storeroom just down the way and you'll see something brilliantly funny.'

'Sorry, can't,' said Sara, shaking her head.

Memphis put on a spooky voice. 'Madame Sockradamus has made her prediction for Sara, remember?'

Sam groaned. 'You're going to spend breather hanging around the sports hall on the off-chance something happens?'

'*Whatever* happens, it'll help me make up my mind about foretelling the future,' said Sara. 'One way or the other.'

'Well, good luck with the good luck,' he said. 'Oi, Thomas! Fido! Come with me . . . You'll like this.'

He led them outside, slowly so that Thomas could keep up. 'Someone is going to have the most awesome trick played on them,' said Sam. 'Down by this storeroom . . . '

The door was still ajar. The trap was as yet unsprung.

Thomas looked blank. 'What's supposed to happen?'

'Hang on, there's Baz,' said Sam, sighting the bad-haired, big-nosed joker lurking shiftily

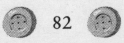

across the corridor. 'Hey, Baz!' he called. 'Any sign of . . . ?'

Sam started miming someone with a really big head. But as he swept his arms out, he smacked someone rushing past in the face. The person flinched away and Sam jumped in alarm—pushing into Fido. Fido clutched hold of Thomas, but Thomas's bad ankle wouldn't support him. He overbalanced and fell . . .

Right into the storeroom door.

'No!' yelled Sam.

But it was too late. The carefully balanced paint pots plopped from the top of the door and splashed all over Thomas.

'Ugh!' he shouted, as the last pot struck him right on the head.

The crowds passing by burst out into gales of laughter at the sight of Thomas Doughty sitting in the doorway, all covered in paint.

Blue paint and black paint.

'Sam,' gasped Fido. 'He's black and blue all over!'

'I know,' said Sam shakily. Suddenly, the joke wasn't so funny.

'I don't believe it!' wailed Thomas.

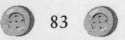

'They don't call him Doubting Thomas for nothing,' Fido muttered.

They helped him up, trying to grab hold of the few bits of him that weren't a dripping, painty mess.

'Let's get him to the boys' bogs quick before we get blamed for this and have to clean it up,' said Sam.

'Looks like Little Knit's prediction has come true all right,' said Fido. 'Just for the wrong person! Left black and blue by the end of the day . . . This trick was meant for you, Sam!'

'But that can't be!' Sam protested. 'Baz said his trap was meant for a dumb, irritating big-headed kid who really fancies himself . . . ' He felt himself blushing. 'Where *is* Baz? The cheek of it, getting me to help him . . . I'll kill him!'

But Baz had disappeared.

'Why would someone I've never seen before go to all that trouble to play a trick on me?' Sam wondered. 'And how did Ginger know it would happen?'

Fido shrugged. 'She predicted the future?'

'Doubt it,' said Thomas. 'I keep telling you, it's just coincidence.'

'What are the chances of so many coincidences happening in a single day?' protested Fido.

'Well,' said Sam, 'this *is* Freekham High—remember?'

Sara and Memphis hung around the sports hall for what felt like ages.

'Breather's nearly over,' said Memphis, checking her watch for about the billionth time. 'Nothing's going to happen now.'

'I suppose you're right,' said Sara.

'And Little Knit was wrong,' said Memphis firmly. 'Oh, well. I need the loo before English. Coming?'

Sara shook her head. 'I've waited this long, I may as well see it through till the end.'

Memphis shrugged. 'OK. Catch you in Bedfellow's class.'

Sara waved her off, and slumped back against the wall of the sports hall, just beside the entrance. A couple of older guys came out through the double doors, hauling between them a big trolley full of sports equipment. They dragged it up the sloping walkway in the direction of the playing fields. Stuff for Sports Day, no doubt. Not long to go now . . .

Then suddenly one of the lads stumbled and fell.

'You tripped me!' he cried.

'You fell over my foot!' his mate retorted. 'Get up, quick! I can't hold it by myself!'

'Do you need a hand?' Sara asked, starting forwards.

'Look out,' he gasped as she approached. 'I can't hold it!'

True to his word, he let go. The loaded trolley started rolling down the slope towards Sara at alarming speed.

Desperately, she threw herself out of the way. But the hard metal edge of the trolley caught her on the shin as she fell, and she gave a howl of pain so loud it was actually embarrassing. *So much for good luck!* she thought. Moments later, the trolley collided with the wall in a cacophonous crash.

'Are you all right?' asked the boy who had fallen. 'Have you hurt anything?'

'My knee, my tights, and my dignity,' Sara answered. She hitched up her skirt a little way

86

to reveal a large, livid lump on her knee. 'Deeply attractive.'

'Can you stand?' he asked, helping her up.

'Just about,' she winced. 'But I don't fancy my chances in the 1500 or the hurdles this afternoon.'

'That's a downer,' he said, and turned back to his friend, the boy who had let go of the trolley. 'You stupid div! Look what you've done!'

The boy came forward. He had an awful bleached-blond mullet, a fat, bulbous nose, and lips like thick, pink slugs. Just for a moment, Sara thought she caught a smirk lurking there.

'Next time, Baz,' the boy said, 'watch where you're putting your dumb feet.'

'Yeah, I will,' said Baz. 'Still, at least it gets you out of Sports Day, right, girlie?'

She frowned at him. 'And that's your apology?'

'It's not my fault.' He shrugged. 'I lost my grip!'

'I've lost my grip on reality even coming here,' Sara muttered. 'You shall have good luck—huh!'

She turned and hobbled away.

'I guess maybe it's just not your lucky day,' she heard Baz call after her.

Periods Five and Six
Double English

Sara staggered down the busy hallways towards Miss Bedfellow's room. When the freaky Freekham hooter sounded for the end of breather, its mad, complaining boom pretty much summed up the way she was feeling. She'd been short-changed by a sock, and she was going to take it up with Ginger in no uncertain terms.

But she found she would have to get in line.

A kid from the year below with close-cropped hair and a lisp was haranguing Ginger. Sock-girl kept looking over at Vicki Starling—probably anxious at the thought of losing the it-girl's approval. Vicki herself was staring wistfully into space, 'emotionally exhausted', no doubt. Whatever.

'I don't get it!' the younger boy was saying crossly. 'You come rushing over to find me at the start of breather. Your dumb sock tells me

 88

that fate will save me from having to run in Sports Day if I hang out by the caretaker's hut. So I hang out there the whole of breather and what happens? Nothing! So, when I come last this afternoon and everyone laughs it's going to be your fault!'

'Look, I'm sorry, Leslie, OK?' said Ginger, pulling Little Knit onto her right hand and still sending worried glances over to Vicki. 'Maybe you didn't wait there long enough.'

'Maybe you're just a big fake and a fraud,' said Leslie, stomping off in a huff.

'I'll second that,' said Sara, crossly limping up to her. 'I stood around outside the sports hall and—'

'Sara, you have to give me a minute,' Ginger said, as she straightened out Little Knit onto her wrist. 'Please?'

The skinny little girl looked so earnest and pathetic that Sara simply nodded and took a step back.

'Vicki Starling!' squawked Ginger in her sock voice. 'It is I, Little Knit!'

Vicki looked up languidly. 'What do you want now, Ginger?'

'It is not Ginger who speaks, but I!' cried the sock indignantly. 'And I have another prophecy. Never mind what Big Stitch said this morning about your true love . . .'

Vicki frowned, and her Chic Clique clone club frowned with her, as if they were different heads of the same animal.

'Never *mind*?' asked Therese, her shocked question a sensible one for once.

'No,' said Little Knit. 'Because, Vicki, you are *truly* meant to be with the *next* person to walk in through *that* door!'

Vicki gasped, and her friends followed suit.

Like everyone else, Sara turned and watched the door like a hawk.

A breathless hush fell.

And then Sam fell through the doorway, stamping and staggering with all the grace of a pregnant monkey shaking a cow pat off its foot.

'It's Sam!' cried Therese, as she often did these days.

'Watch where you're going, mate!' shouted Sam at someone out of sight beyond the door. 'I almost tripped over you!'

'So it's true!' sighed Vicki. 'Truly true!'

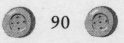

'It's true twice over, sweetie!' gasped Denise.

'I knew you two were made for each other,' beamed Elise.

'I did too!' said Therese quickly.

Sara shook her head. 'Oh, brother.'

'You can say that again,' croaked Ginger, pulling Little Knit from her sweaty hand.

'What's wrong with you lot now?' asked Sam, baffled.

'Sam,' said Vicki, her eyes wide and glistening. 'You're my destiny!'

'Not again,' he groaned. 'Look, if this is another of Little Knit's predictions, I'm here to tell you it's bound to be rubbish.'

Vicki smiled at her friends. 'He's such a kidder!'

'Well, this is no joke,' said Sara, showing Ginger her gammy leg. 'You told me I'd have good luck at breather if I stood outside the sports hall. Instead, I got sideswiped by a runaway trolley!'

'And you said I'd end up black and blue by the end of the day,' added Sam. 'Well, I haven't.' He glanced back through the doorway. 'But *Thomas* has!'

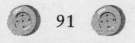

Sara stared as Fido helped Doubting Thomas into the classroom. His clothes were covered in blue and black paint. His face and hands were red and sore from where he had scrubbed at the stains.

Ginger slumped to her seat, and looked as if she might cry. 'It's not my fault,' she complained. 'Everything's going wrong—and all because Big Stitch was socknapped!'

'Rubbish,' said Doubting Thomas. 'There's something you're not telling us, Ginger. What is it?'

Ginger sobbed and pulled out an envelope from her skirt pocket. 'This letter was left in my locker. I just found it. It's from the socknapper!'

'What does it say?' asked Sara, intrigued despite herself.

'It says I have to go to the bike sheds at lunchtime if I want to get Big Stitch back. And look!' She emptied out the envelope into Sara's hand.

A strip of stripy fabric flopped into her outstretched palm. It looked to be about half of Big Stitch's woollen tongue.

'No wonder my prophecies are coming out garbled,' she sighed.

 92

'Hey, Sam!' called Vicki. 'What she said about *us* isn't garbled. What are you doing at lunchtime—want to hang with us?'

I'd sooner hang myself, he thought. 'Vicki, how can you like me just because a sock says so?'

'*Two* socks say so,' said Denise, triumphantly, and the other girls nodded in unanimous agreement.

Just then, Memphis strode in through the door. 'Bedfellow's on her way,' she announced.

Sam stopped Sara as she headed for her chair. 'This letter, and the chopped off tongue trick . . . You think it's all down to this bloke who's been hassling her, Carl Witlow?'

'Well, he's mean enough and ugly enough,' Sara agreed. 'And he seems to have it in for Ginger. Maybe that's why she's messed up her predictions . . . '

'Predictions, pah! It's all a load of rubbish,' said Thomas Doughty.

Fido looked at him with a mixture of despair and admiration. 'What's it going to take to convince you that there's something in this prediction stuff?'

'There's nothing that *can* convince me,' he said stoutly. 'It's coincidence. Or it's a trick. That's all.'

As Sara limped over to where Memphis sat, mulling over his words, Miss Bedfellow came in. She was a confident, sassy-looking woman in a smart black suit. Her sharp nose was held high in the air, and long frizzy dark curls streamed out behind her as she strode to her desk.

'Shut up, you lot,' she said briskly, picking up a sheaf of papers. 'Now, continuing our work on how great love inspires great writing, today we shall look at how poets deal with love's first beginnings . . . '

'It's how *Sam's* going to deal with it I want to know!' said Sara as she eased herself painfully into her seat.

'I can't leave you alone for a minute, can I?' said Memphis. 'What happened to you?'

'It's weird,' hissed Sara. 'Some kid called Leslie is told by Ginger to wait around the caretaker's hut, right? If he does that, she says, something will happen to him that will get him out of Sports Day.'

'And what happens?' asked Memphis.

'Nothing. He waits around, and fat zilch.'

 94

'Little Knit loses a point.'

'*Two* points,' said Sara. 'Because while I'm waiting around the sports hall for good luck to strike, a dirty great trolley strikes first. Whacks into my legs, and puts me out of action—so now *I* can't make Sports Day.'

Memphis looked at her steadily with those amazing sea-green eyes. 'Coincidence?'

'Or a mix-up. Maybe if Leslie had gone to the sports hall he'd be happily rubbing his shin and thanking his lucky stars, while I . . . '

'You'd have spent breather outside the care-taker's hut,' said Memphis. 'For nothing.'

'Maybe I'd have found something meant for me that Leslie didn't!'

Memphis gave her a look. 'Sara, that's like when you buy a scratchcard and you don't win anything, and you think—well, if I buy *another* scratchcard, *that* will be the lucky one. It won't.'

'You've changed your tune,' Sara argued. 'You seemed ready enough to believe, before.'

Memphis pulled a face. 'That was before I real-ized I was buying into the same stuff as Vicki Starling. I mean, come on!'

'Ladies, could you wrap up the chat?' Bedfellow

 95

looked over at them warningly. 'I'm trying to take a lesson here.'

'Sorry, miss,' said Sara. She liked Miss Bedfellow, she was kind of cool. For a teacher.

'Make it up to me by handing out these photo-copied poems.' She thrust the papers in Sara's direction.

Sara duly traipsed around the class handing them out.

'Now, who wants to read our first poem?' Bedfellow asked, peering from face to grimacing face. 'No one? All right, then, you'll all have to read a bit each.'

A mumbled moaning started up.

'And don't start. Anyone messing around today can stand straight outside that door,' said Bedfellow firmly. 'I've got a headache and I'm not in the mood for interup—'

Before she could finish the word, she was inter-rupted. A heavy knock at the door signalled the arrival of a familiar, surly figure with a square jaw and piggy little eyes.

'Carl Witlow,' sighed Miss Bedfellow, massag-ing the bridge of her nose as if her headache had just got worse.

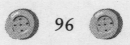

Sara saw Sam turn to frown at her. There was a questioning look on his face.

She nodded and whispered: 'That's him!'

Sam stared at the guy. So *this* was Carl Witlow. It was the same guy he'd tripped over outside the classroom. But Sam felt he should remember him from somewhere else, as well . . .

Clearly, so did Vicki Starling. 'Oh, not *him*,' she muttered, and mimed a finger down her throat. Her clone club copied her in synchronized motion.

Carl just stood there. Sam wondered what this guy had done to offend Vicki—and whether he might share the secrets of his success with Sam.

'You should be in class, Carl,' said Bedfellow. 'What do you want?'

'Sorry, miss,' he grunted. 'School office sent me. They've got an urgent phone call for Ginger Mutton.'

Ginger emitted a strangled squeak.

So that was why Carl had been hanging around outside the classroom, thought Sam: waiting for the chance to get at Ginger . . .

'All right, Ginger, you'd better go,' said Miss

Bedfellow. 'Don't worry, we'll save a line for you to read.'

'Yes, miss.' She looked pained and miserable, more as if she was going off to her doom than skipping some of class to answer the phone.

And probably with good reason, thought Sam. Carl had a cruel smile on his face; this phone call thing had to be bogus. So what did he really want with Ginger? He'd hassled her twice already according to Sara . . . But what could be so urgent he had to steal her out of a lesson for the chance to talk?

Sam had the feeling there was a lot more to this than met the eye—even the single button eye of Little Knit. Loving a good mystery, he knew he had to get out there himself and listen in for the sake of his own curiosity . . .

'Right,' said Bedfellow, as Ginger followed Carl glumly from the classroom and the door closed behind her. 'The first poem is "First Love" by John Clare, seventeen ninety-three to eighteen sixty-four. Vicki, you can start us off.'

Sam scanned the poem. Yuck—very lovey-dovey. He had to get out fast. Maybe he could pretend he was going to throw up?

Then, inspiration struck. Bedfellow was in a bad mood, it shouldn't take much to light her fuse . . .

Vicki cleared her delicate throat and, with a coy look in Sam's direction, began to read:

'I ne'er was struck before that hour
With love so sudden and so sweet
Her face it bloomed like a sweet flower—'

'Shame about her smelly feet,' said Sam loudly.

The class broke out in hysterics, but Bedfellow wasn't laughing. 'I warned you, Sam,' she said wearily. 'Get outside.'

'Thanks, miss!' beamed Sam, and he ran for the door.

The moment he got outside, he found Ginger just a few metres down the corridor, with Carl Witlow towering over her.

'Hey, Ginge,' Sam called. 'Thought you had a phone call to take?'

'She's taken it,' growled Carl with a filthy look in his direction.

'Pretty short call,' said Sam. 'Wrong number?'

But Carl had turned back to Ginger. 'Just get Big Stitch back by the end of lunchtime and stop messing up the predictions,' he said, jabbing a

99

finger into her shoulder. 'Or your life won't be worth living. I'll check up on you later in the usual place.'

With that, he turned and skulked away.

'Well, well,' Sam muttered. 'So Witlow's *not* the socknapper!'

Ginger turned back towards Sam, her eyes red and blotchy with tears through her thick glasses. 'What are you doing out here? Haven't you done enough damage?'

'Damage?' Sam frowned. 'The only thing I'm trying to break is the world record for being sent out of class the most times in a single day.' He softened his voice. 'But don't worry. I shan't ask your socks to rate my chances.'

'You don't believe, do you?' said Ginger. 'No one's going to believe me unless I get Big Stitch back.'

'What's to believe?' Sam looked her straight in the eye. 'Ginger, I don't know how you've been doing it, but it's all just a trick, isn't it? A fix?'

'You'll never understand, Sam,' she sighed, and brushed past him back into the classroom.

Lunchtime

Bedfellow wasn't as evil as Horrible Hayes, not by a long way. She let Sam back into the class after only ten minutes.

'Sorry, miss,' he'd said. 'It's just my sense of humour.'

She'd half-smiled. 'Since that's the only sense you have, I suppose I can't be too hard on you.'

She settled for making him read an extra-slushy poem all by himself. Vicki Starling hung on his every word as if he was speaking straight to her. Now that two freaky fortune-telling socks had named Sam as her true love, it was going to take cruelty of earth-shattering proportions to put her off him. And Sam wasn't the cruel kind, not really.

So what was he going to do?

When the siren sounded for lunch, and Bedfellow stalked from the room in search of

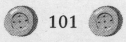 101

painkillers, Ginger was hot on her heels. But Sam's heart sank when he saw that Vicki and her gaggle of girlfriends were in no hurry to go anywhere else. They made a beeline for him.

'Sam, you read that love poem so beautifully,' said Elise. She looked between him and Vicki. 'You were thinking of someone in particular, weren't you?'

'Yep—me,' Sam admitted. 'I just love me to bits.'

The girls giggled, and Vicki looked straight at him. 'That's not so hard to understand.'

Sam felt himself going red. 'Vicki, how can you say that—you hardly know me!'

'That's because you keep pushing me away,' she complained. 'Are you afraid of getting hurt?'

'Should I be?' He looked at her worriedly. 'Do you do judo or something?'

'Sam, I've made up my mind,' said Vicki, closing in. 'And I think we need to give this thing a try.'

'Vicki, until the sock put my name in the frame, you acted like I wasn't alive!'

'That was then, this is now,' said Elise. 'Run with it, Sam.'

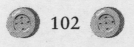

102

'I don't like running,' said Sam. 'That's why I got out of Sports Day.'

'Then stop running away from me,' said Vicki. She straightened and blew him a kiss. 'Now, I think it's time I made you cooler by showing you off to all my friends.'

Sam stared at her in horror. 'Huh?'

She looked at her Chic Clique and rolled her eyes in an *Isn't he dumb but cute?* kind of way. 'We're just going to freshen up a little, then we're going to do a walk-round of all our cool pals and do the introductions.'

'Her devoted true love,' sighed Therese.

'Her dude of destiny,' added Denise.

Elise beamed. 'The guy of her dreams.'

Sam screwed up his nose. 'Who *are* all these blokes?'

'You're such a kidder, Sam,' said Vicki happily. 'We'll meet you outside the canteen in fifteen.'

'Be there,' said Elise.

'Or we'll come looking,' Denise promised.

'So, TTFN!' said Therese. 'That means Ta-Ta For Now.'

'Not on this occasion,' said Sam weakly as the

103

girls walked away, arm in arm. 'It means, Totally Traumatized, Feeling Nauseous.'

He turned to see Sara limping over to his desk, Memphis just behind her.

'Help,' he said feebly.

'Is it safe to talk to you now?' Sara enquired acidly. 'Or do we need to make an appointment with your social secretaries?'

'Yeah, what's it like to have your own fan club?' added Memphis, an amused smile playing around her lips.

'I'm going into hiding,' Sam announced. 'I can't take this. I'm going to sneak off somewhere secret and hope that all of this goes away.' He noticed Fido and Thomas Doughty heading for the door. 'Hey, guys, want to hang out in the music block?'

'That's closed for redecoration,' frowned Sara. 'No one's allowed in.'

'Exactly,' grinned Sam. 'Should make a good hideout!'

'Sorry, Sam,' said Thomas. 'Last minute Sports Day training calls.'

'But you're not doing any running!'

'The training's for me,' said Fido.

Thomas smiled. 'I don't believe he's in shape. I'm going to show him how to warm up properly.'

Memphis smiled. 'Like Vicki's going to show *you*, Sam, when she catches up with you . . . '

'Never mind that,' said Sara quickly, as Fido and Thomas left the room. 'What happened with Ginger and Carl?'

Sam told them the few scraps of info he'd learned, and about the mysterious Baz who set traps for strangers.

'So then, the socknapper's note *didn't* come from Carl,' said Sara. 'And how does this Baz guy factor into the whole deal?'

'I don't know,' said Sam. 'But if Ginger doesn't get the sock back by the end of lunchtime, Carl Witlow is threatening all kinds of stuff.'

'Poor old Ginger,' said Sara. 'I feel kind of bad for her. She only wants to be liked.'

'It's her sock that's popular, not her,' said Sam. 'Maybe that's why someone's pinched it—they want to set up their own fortune telling act!'

'Enough of the mights and maybes,' said Sara. 'I think we should go check out the bike sheds. That anonymous note told Ginger to wait there, remember?'

'I'm with Sara,' said Sam. 'I hate unsolved mysteries.'

'I thought you were going into hiding?' said Memphis.

'I am,' said Sam. He smiled. 'So you do all the legwork, then come and find me in the music block and tell me all about it, OK?'

Sara rolled her eyes. 'Come on, Memph. Let's leave the love god here to his vanishing act—and get to it!'

A short while later, Sara was hobbling determinedly towards the bike sheds with Memphis in tow. Ginger was some way ahead of them, walking briskly with a petite Asian girl.

'Who's she?' asked Sara.

'Looks like Mindy Murthy,' said Memphis. 'One of Ginger's old crowd she hung around with. Kind of a "dweebs stick together" thing.'

'Ginger was crying on Mindy's shoulder at break this morning, in the toilets,' Sara recalled. 'Mindy was warning her she'd get into trouble if she carried on with her fortune telling. And it looks like she was right.'

'Don't tell me,' said Memphis. 'She can see the future too.'

They kept pushing on towards the bike sheds as fast as Sara's leg would allow.

Ginger and Mindy were looking around but there was no sign of anyone waiting there, nor of anyone else coming to meet them. The two girls started poking about the place, searching through gleaming racers and rusted old heaps.

Mindy noticed Memphis and Sara approaching and looked at them doubtfully. But then Ginger found something. She jumped in the air with a cheer.

'Big Stitch!' she shouted. 'I've found Big Stitch!'

Sara frowned. 'What, it was just lying here, waiting to be found?'

'He was tied up under this saddle,' said Ginger, pressing the sock to her cheek.

Memphis was puzzled too. 'So, no ransom demand? No threatening behaviour?'

Mindy was eyeing them mistrustfully. 'Do you know these people, Ginge?'

'They're in my class,' said Ginger vaguely, cradling her sock as if it was her little baby. 'Oh,

Big Stitch! I'll get your eye back from Little Knit and we'll fix up your tongue . . . '

'And then I'd put Little Knit back on your foot before you get Big Blisters from running around sockless,' suggested Memphis.

'Why did you have to make another sock puppet so quickly anyway, Ginger?' asked Mindy. 'Couldn't you at least *try* to get by without a sock on your hand, even for a few hours?'

Ginger gave her a dark look. 'See ya, Mindy. I've got stuff to do.'

'Why don't you come and hang with me and the guys?' Mindy suggested hopefully. 'We never see you any more.'

'Sorry, I can't,' said Ginger. 'I have to go stitch up Big Stitch.'

'Big Stitch is the one stitching *you* up!' shouted Mindy. 'You think you need him as a crutch, but you don't!'

But Ginger had already run off in a sulk. She was a speedy little thing. Mindy stared after her for a few moments. Then she stuck her hands in her pockets and marched off in the opposite direction.

Sara watched them go, and then turned to Memphis. 'That stinks,' she sighed.

'What, the sock?' joked Memphis.

'The way it's squashed their friendship,' said Sara.

'Not to mention the way it's wasted our time. I reckon the only things that should be worn on the wrists are sleeve cuffs and bracelets.'

Sara felt a moment's sadness for her own beloved bracelet, thrown out by her dozy dad and now lost for ever. 'You know, that socknapping thing just doesn't make sense. Why go to all the trouble of stealing Big Stitch just to give it straight back again?'

'Maybe they got cold feet about the whole thing.'

'They should have worn Big Stitch,' said Sara. 'Then at least *one* foot would be warm!'

With nothing else happening at the sheds, they headed back to the playground.

Sam had sneaked around the back of the music block. It was a small, low outbuilding set towards the far end of the school grounds, with very little human traffic passing by.

He was deciding how best to breach the building—should he try the door or sneak in through the window?—when he had a strange feeling of being watched.

He turned round and found the feeling wasn't so strange after all. He *was* being watched. From beneath the badly bleached fringe of an unspeakable mullet.

Baz must have been following him. Now he was walking his way. No one else was in sight.

Sam folded his arms as the bigger lad squared up to him. 'Let me guess—you found me by the size of my head, right? It must be bigger than ever since I dodged your little prank so easily. Maybe I'm not as dumb as you've been told.'

'You're definitely as irritating,' Baz countered.

'I ought to split on you,' said Sam. 'I'll bet Penter would love to know that you're responsible for that painty mess all over the storeroom.'

'Uh-uh.' Baz shook his head. 'Not *me*, Innocent. *Us*. That's why I got you to help once you'd seen what I was up to—so you'd be involved too.'

'Clever. But why did you want to get me soaked in paint, anyway?' Sam demanded. 'Did Ginger put you up to it, to make her prediction come true?'

'No,' said Baz. 'But it's not too late.' He smiled

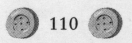

110

and clenched his fists. 'There are other ways to make you black and blue.'

Sam checked around, but he was alone. No pupils, no teachers—no witnesses. He felt his heart start to race.

'Come on, Baz,' he said. 'Don't do something I'll regret, eh?'

'I'm just here to warn you to stay away,' said Baz.

'Who from—your barber?'

'From Vicki Starling, smart-arse.'

'Vicki?' Sam frowned. 'What are you on about?'

'You know what I'm on about. Everyone knows she's crazy for you.'

'Well, she's only human.'

Baz grabbed hold of Sam's school tie and twisted it. 'Leave her alone, Innocent.'

'I'm trying to!' gasped Sam, half-throttled. 'Not that it's any of your business.'

'Just take my advice, mate. If you keep on after Vicki Starling, there'll be trouble.' Baz let go of Sam's tie and pushed him back against the wall. 'And sock or no sock, that's one prediction that's gonna come true.'

Sam watched him go, his fingers clawing at the knot of his tie. It had been tightened to about the size of a peanut.

Now that Baz had gone, Sam felt a sudden surge of anger through his fear. What was the guy's problem? How dare he tell Sam who he could and couldn't see! Was he jealous or something?

For a moment he thought about going after Baz and teaching him a lesson. But since the lesson would probably be 'How best to beat up someone smaller than yourself'—with Sam as the practice dummy—a moment later he decided to stick to plan A: hide from the world and hope it went away.

Carefully, he pulled open a window that had been left ajar to let out paint fumes. Then he quietly clambered inside the music block.

As soon as Sam got inside, he heard voices from somewhere close by. He froze. Teachers?

No. Ginger Mutton and Carl Witlow, in the corridor outside. What were *they* doing here?

He tiptoed over to the door and listened in.

'So you got the sock back, OK, that's good,' said Carl. 'And you can fix it up, that's fine. But you've got to fix its reputation too, and fast. Have you got the note with those predictions on?'

'Yes, it's still stitched into his lining,' said Ginger.

'Good. Because I want Vicki Starling sorted out by afternoon registration. I've got something special planned for her.' There was a pause. 'And don't forget, Mutton—any more mess-ups and I'll put you back among the Z-crowd where you belong.'

Sam's eyes widened. So Ginger didn't have an accomplice after all. She had a stage-manager—Carl. But why?

His mind started wrestling with the pieces of the puzzle, trying to make some sense of them all. Then he heard heavy footsteps moving away back down the corridor, followed by the sound of Ginger's snuffling sobs.

He waited till he was certain she was alone, then slowly opened the door. He could see her, tear-stained and bedraggled, sitting cross-legged on the floor with a needle and thread, sewing a button onto Big Stitch's 'face'.

The door suddenly gave a protesting creak.

Ginger looked up in alarm and gasped as she saw him.

'How long have you been there?' she demanded.

'Long enough to overhear your little chat with Carl,' said Sam.

'It's not how you think it is,' she said taking off her glasses and wiping them on her sleeve.

'Oh yeah?' he asked. 'So how about you explain how it *really* is?'

'What's the point?' she hissed, getting quickly to her feet and plonking her glasses back on the end of her nose. 'You wouldn't believe me anyway.'

'Try me,' said Sam.

But Ginger was already stomping off towards the music block's main doors. 'I haven't got time. I have to give some predictions before I meet up with Cass Shaw later on.'

'You do that! I'm sure she'd love to know what a fraud you are!' Sam called after her. 'What are you and Carl planning for Vicki Starling, huh? What are these prophecies he's told you to say?'

But Ginger kept on going. Until she ran into Sara and Memphis as they slipped through the

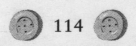

main doors. They stood side by side, blocking her way out.

'Those sound like good questions to me, Ginger,' said Sara. 'Do you have good answers?'

Ginger turned back the way she'd come, to find Sam walking towards her. 'Why should I tell you anything?'

'Because I've been threatened, harassed, assaulted, cajoled, wooed, falsely accused, yelled at and very nearly covered in paint as a result of your sock's predictions,' said Sam. 'And I'd like to know what it's all been for!'

'Seems to me like you're in trouble, Ginger,' said Sara. 'Maybe we could help.'

Ginger heaved an enormous sigh and leaned back against the wall. 'Everything's just gone so *weird*.'

'You may as well give up to them, Ginge,' said Memphis. 'When it comes to weird stuff, these guys can't leave it alone. I reckon it's their destiny, you know?'

'Destiny?' asked Ginger uncertainly.

'What goes around comes around—that's what they say, isn't it?' Memphis gave her a knowing smile. 'Well, I reckon freaky stuff has gone on

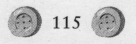 115

around here since the world began. And since our leap-year twins both started here on the same day, they've brought the weird stuff coming around all over again. So maybe they can help stop it.'

Ginger looked between Sam on one side and Sara on the other.

And she slumped her shoulders, and nodded.

'I wasn't making up that stuff about ley lines,' said Ginger, as they all sat together in a room freshly painted an unsettling shade of puce. 'Or about Big Stitch being made from gypsy wool.'

'From a gypsy sheep?' wondered Sam.

Sara chushed him.

'I started up Big Stitch as a kind of joke for my friends. But sometimes, you know, I do get ideas. Sort of, feelings.' She looked at Sara. 'You know, about people, and what might happen if they got together. But it was easy to predict the future of my bunch of friends—Mindy, Deborah, Beth . . . ' She slipped on Big Stitch and spoke in his voice. 'You will be bored and ignored for the rest of your lives and have no nice boys fancying you, the end.'

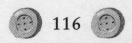

'Bit harsh, isn't it?' said Sam.

Ginger sighed. 'It's just the way it is.'

Memphis looked at her. 'So you and your sock took an interest in the cooler kids, right?' Sara couldn't tell if her green eyes held amusement or disapproval.

'When you're a geek,' said Ginger, 'you get kind of obsessed with the cooler kids. I watched them, and I could just tell who were right for each other and who weren't.'

'And so you went up and told them,' said Sam.

'I was too shy to speak to them by myself,' Ginger admitted. 'I've always been shy, and I hate it. But with Big Stitch on my wrist, doing my act, I'm more confident. It's like . . . I'm a different person.'

'Yeah, you are,' said Sam. 'But that different person is a sock. Didn't the A-crowd just laugh in your face?'

'At first.'

'Did they tell you to "shoe"?'

'Shut up,' Sara warned him. 'Go on, Ginger.'

'It was awful,' she said quietly. 'I wanted the ground to swallow me up. But I guess afterwards they got thinking, and saw that maybe there was something in what we had said. For starters, I got Kirsten Cowley and Mike Regan together.'

'Then you hit the jackpot with Cassie Shaw and John Pidgin,' said Memphis.

'Uh-huh. They were the dream team,' Ginger agreed. 'Once I got *them* together, Jenny Moon actually came to *me* for advice.'

Memphis nodded. 'And you fixed her up with Rob Baron.'

'I just told her who she was compatible with,' said Ginger. 'Sometimes people need a push in the right direction.'

'OK,' said Sara, 'so word spread about you and your sock being queen of the matchmakers, right?'

'People actually remembered my name,' said Ginger, smiling distantly. 'Came up to me and started talking.'

'Or rather *asking*. Asking your sock to tell them about themselves and their love matches.'

'My old friends didn't understand,' said Ginger. 'They were just jealous 'cause suddenly I was hanging with Cassie and Kirsten and the rest.'

'Hanging with them?' snorted Memphis. 'They're using you, that's all!'

'It's better than nothing!' Ginger insisted.

'But I don't get it,' said Sam. 'If you were just playing the geek-chic queen of hearts thing, how did this whole spooky prediction thing get started?'

'I told you, I sometimes get feelings about things,' said Ginger, her watery eyes wide and spooky behind her thick glasses. 'It's like I suddenly know what's going to happen next . . . '

'Yeah, it's easy to predict the future if you already know what's going to happen,' Sam argued. 'You and Carl have been fixing prophecies between you. But why?'

'Carl came up to me after school one day last week,' said Ginger distantly. 'He told me that the cool kids would soon get bored with me. That they'd dump me right back where I came from. I knew he was right . . . But then he said that he had thought up a way to make me popular. To make everyone think I was totally amazing.'

'With a full-on fortune-telling sock,' Sara realized.

Ginger nodded. 'Till now, no one guessed that me and Carl even know each other. We normally meet around here, out of everyone's way.' She sighed. 'Carl and his mate have been arranging little stunts and setting people up. He gives me a list of predictions I have to make—then he makes sure they happen.'

'Why make so many predictions about Doubting Thomas Doughty?' wondered Sam.

'Carl thought that if we could make him believe in Big Stitch, it would persuade other people to believe,' she said. 'So when I told Thomas that trouble was afoot, Carl stole one of his trainers from the changing rooms. When I said he would have some bad luck when the full moon fell, Carl's mate dropped a bar of soap in his path—'

'And made sure there was a bag with a full moon logo hanging nearby,' Sam concluded. 'Clever.'

'Those were mean things to do to him,' said Sara. 'He could have been hurt.'

'I . . . I know,' sighed Ginger. 'But I'm in too deep with Carl to stop. That's why I made up that prediction about Thomas being lucky in love. It was me who planted that five pound note under his desk when we studied *Romeo and Juliet* . . . '

'Big deal,' said Sam crossly. 'You bung him a fiver to make yourself feel less guilty. But you never did manage to convince him, did you?'

'The stunts helped to make other people believe in Big Stitch,' said Ginger shiftily. 'So Carl was happy.'

'Oh, good for him,' said Sara. 'What about poor old Fido? He wasn't so happy when he got that bad grade on his homework.'

Ginger shrugged. 'I didn't know anything about that.'

Sam looked at her doubtfully. 'All right, then, how about the Big Chunx trick?'

'One of Carl's mates is Mrs Hurst's son,' said Ginger. 'He knew in advance she was putting Big Chunx on special offer today.'

Memphis clapped her hands. 'And that's how you knew Hurst was going to let her year ten netball team wear their own knickers from now on!'

'Easy when you know how,' remarked Sara.

'This mate of Carl's,' asked Sam. 'Is it a big-nosed bloke with a bad mullet called Baz?'

Ginger nodded sadly. 'Yes, that's him.'

'He was the one preparing the black and blue trap for me,' said Sam. 'Thick-lipped little zero.'

'He sounds like the boy who let that trolley knock into me outside the sports hall!' Sara burst in indignantly. 'How about that, Ginger? How come you sent me off to get injured like that—I could have been badly hurt!'

'I know why,' said Sam. 'She gets Carl to write down the prophecies she has to make, and sticks them into Big Stitch's ankle so she can sneakily read them while she's doing her act. You know what her memory's like! Without a prompt . . . '

Ginger's head drooped down sadly.

'Of course,' said Sara. 'That's why you got me and that Leslie guy mixed up, and sent us to the wrong places.'

'All Carl told Baz was to get someone called Leslie who'd be waiting outside the sports hall, and to make it look like an accident,' said Ginger. 'When he saw you, he must have thought you were a *Lesley*. . . '

'Oh, that's wonderful,' said Sara crossly. 'Ginger, this whole thing has got way out of hand. You see that, right?'

Ginger didn't say anything.

'What I don't understand is *why* Carl is helping you,' said Sam. 'What's in it for him?

Why does he try so hard to convince Vicki Starling that I'm the man of her dreams—and then send Baz along to warn me to stay away from her, or else?'

'Oh . . . that,' said Ginger forlornly. 'Everything Carl has done, he's done because of Vicki. Carl is crazy about her. He's hassled her to go out with him for months but she doesn't want to know.'

Memphis prodded Sara in the ribs. 'We heard her talking about a psycho in the year above, remember?'

'That's why he's been working so hard to build up Big Stitch's reputation,' said Ginger miserably. 'My sock had to seem so completely right about everything, that no one could believe he could get anything wrong. And then Sam messed everything up!' She pulled off her glasses and wiped her teary eyes on her sleeve. 'Carl was waiting outside the classroom door this morning, ready to walk inside at a set time as Vicki's true love. I'd built everything up—'

'And then Sam came dashing in!' cried Memphis, cupping her hands over her mouth. 'Ouch!'

Sam was wincing too. 'How was I to know? I was late, I was in a big rush, I just shot past him!'

'So Carl came and found me afterwards to make me read out some more predictions,' said Ginger.

'No wonder he wanted to leave me black and blue,' said Sam. 'I blundered in and stole his thunder.'

'Not once, but twice,' Sara realized. 'You tried to get Vicki to believe her *real* true love was coming into class after breather—and Sam burst in on the act again!'

'*That's* what Carl was doing outside the classroom,' Sam groaned, slapping a hand to his forehead. 'Waiting to make his big entrance!'

Ginger glared at him. 'And you tripped over him just as he was ready to stride in and steal her heart.'

'Steal is right,' said Memphis. 'I doubt she'd give it willingly, sock or no sock.'

'That's why you cobbled together Little Knit when Big Stitch got socknapped,' breathed Sara. 'You needed *something* to make those extra predictions!'

'But who did the socknapping?' said Sam.

 124

'And why?' added Sara.

'I don't care,' said Ginger. 'The only thing that matters is that I've got Big Stitch back again.' She turned his 'neck' inside out to reveal a piece of paper pinned there. 'And I've still got Carl's prompts pinned to the lining so I won't mix up his predictions for the day. There are some I have to make this lunchtime . . . '

Sara stared at her. 'You're going on with this mad set-up?'

'I *have* to,' whined Ginger. 'If I don't, Carl will expose me! He'll tell the world that Big Stitch is a Big Fake and no one cool will want me around ever again.'

'Your real friends will *always* stand by you, Ginger,' said Sara. 'If you'll only let them.'

'I like my new friends,' Ginger insisted. 'Like Cass Shaw. She wants me to meet her at the end of lunch . . . And meantime, Carl wants Vicki off Sam and into him by afternoon registration!'

'Suits me,' said Sam. 'If Vicki's dumb enough to let a sock tell her who to like, she deserves a loser like Witlow.'

'But, Ginger, you can't carry on tricking people like this!' Sara argued.

'You're not going to split on me, are you?' asked Ginger, wide-eyed and trembling. 'I thought . . . maybe if you knew what's been going on, you'd understand . . . '

'People are getting hurt,' said Sara. '*I'm* getting hurt!'

'And I'm going to get hurt too if I'm seen so much as looking in Vicki Starling's direction,' Sam complained.

'I know,' said Ginger. 'That's why I thought Sara and Memphis would want to help put Vicki off you—for *your* sake, not for mine!'

'You *are* craftier than you look,' said Sam, almost admiringly. 'What about it, girls?'

Sara looked at Memphis. Memphis shrugged.

'We'll think about it,' said Sara.

'Over lunch,' added Memphis. 'I'm starving.'

'But if we *do* help you, Ginger,' Sara warned, 'today's your last day as a fortune teller—right?'

'Carl won't be bothered about fixing any more predictions once he's hooked Vicki.' She patted the sock puppet on her hand. 'Me and Stitch'll go back to being mystic matchmakers, and no one else will get hurt. 'K?'

'Great in theory,' said Sam. 'But first we'll have to think of a way to put Vicki off me.'

Memphis grinned mysteriously, her green eyes glittering. 'Oh, I think that can be arranged . . . '

So while Sam hid out in fear of a beating—or worse, a round of toe-curling introductions to a bunch of A-crowd bores—Sara and Memphis ate their lunch.

'Crazy, isn't it?' Sara mused through a mouthful of sandwich. 'How this sock thing has grown and grown.'

'It's just a freaky phase,' said Memphis, munching daintily on a forkful of salad. 'It'll soon blow over. That's *my* prediction.'

'I hope you're not planning on getting Carl Witlow to make it come true,' joked Sara. 'What a creep. Does he really think he can trick someone into liking him?'

'Especially when they hate him in the first place,' Memphis agreed. 'I doubt even Vicki Starling is *so* stupid she would think Carl could ever be her true love.'

'Don't be so sure,' said Sara sourly. 'Anyway,

 127

you still haven't told me your plan for putting Vicki off Sam.'

Memphis ate the last of her lunch and smiled slyly. 'It's a surprise.'

'I don't like surprises,' Sara grimaced. 'Whatever it is, if it's going to work by afternoon registration, shouldn't you be springing into action?'

'Oh, it won't take long,' she said airily.

Sara sighed and dumped the rest of her sandwich on her plate. 'I wonder how Ginger's getting on with the rest of her predictions?'

Memphis checked her watch. 'Probably jumping through hoops for her good pal "Cass" and company now, trying to be one of the gang.'

'Maybe they'll *learn* to like her,' said Sara hopefully.

Memphis gave her a funny look. 'And maybe Therese will say something intelligent some day.'

'*Aaaaaaauggghhhhhhhhh!*' came an almighty shriek from the far side of the canteen. It was Therese.

'Not bad, for her,' Memphis conceded.

Therese came squelching their way, her hair and uniform dripping wet.

 128

'What happened?' asked Sara.

'Big Stitch told me that if I went to the canteen I'd make a big splash with this guy I like,' she wailed.

Memphis was trying to cope with an attack of giggles. 'And you . . . uh . . . made a different kind of splash, right?'

'This crazy person came out of the kitchen with a whole basin of water and spilled it all over me!' sobbed Therese. 'I'm wet!'

'You can say that again,' Memphis muttered.

'Never mind,' said Sara, biting her lip to stop her spreading smile. 'Why not go and stand under the warm air dryer in the toilets.'

'I ought to sue!' she moaned, splashing off at the gallop and leaving them with a final tortured wail: 'What if my uniform shrinks?'

'Then it'll be a good match for your brain,' said Memphis.

'But who went crazy with the basin?' wondered Sara, watching as a couple of dinner ladies flapped about with cloths, cleaning up the mess. 'I didn't see that Baz guy anywhere . . . and why would Carl want to upset one of Vicki's clone club, especially now?'

'I'll bet no one did it. Therese is so dopy, she probably walked straight into one of the kitchen cleaners all by herself.' Memphis got up. 'Are you finished? Let's grab some fresh air.'

But stepping outside, a terrible 'country' smell hit their noses.

'Ugh!' groaned Sara. 'What a stink! Like a bunch of cows getting busy after a night spent eating stewed prunes.'

'And that's where it's coming from!' said Memphis. For once, she actually looked shocked.

And Sara soon saw why.

Elise was tottering along the path towards them, apparently in a state of shock. Crowds of people scattered before her, clutching their noses and groaning.

She was covered in manure. It clung to her hair, was smeared on her face, and stuck to her uniform. A small cloud of flies was buzzing around her.

'What happened to *you*?' cried Sara.

'Big Stitch,' she said, in a daze. 'He told me that if I went to the school farm by myself, I'd find everything coming up roses. But when I got there, this big stack of manure fell on me!'

'Therese is in the canteen block toilets,' said

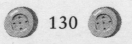 130

Sara quickly, holding her nose. 'Why don't you go join her there? She'll look after you.'

Elise nodded and left without another word.

Sara stared after her in disbelief. 'What is Carl playing at?'

'Looks like Ginger's sock has developed a bitter streak since it got socknapped,' said Memphis. 'Maybe we should go and see what she has to say about it.'

'Cassie Shaw may have collected her from the cloaks by now.'

'No harm in trying.'

But on their way, they passed a fresh commotion. Completing a hat trick of disasters for the Chic Cliquers, Denise came running out shrieking from the Home Ec. Block with what looked like a bowlful of sticky cake mix spilled all over her school jumper and skirt.

'She got off lightly,' murmured Memphis.

'Let me guess,' said Sara as Denise approached. 'Big Stitch told you to go to the cookery rooms?'

'He said something delicious would happen to me if I did,' she said, red-faced and furious. 'And some dweeby little girl tripped and threw *this* lot all over me!'

 131

Memphis swiped a bit with her little finger and sucked the end. 'Well, it's not delicious, but it's certainly not bad.'

Denise huffed and stamped off in a rage.

'Your friends are in the canteen block toilets,' Sara called after her helpfully.

'I'll tell you one thing,' said Denise fiercely. 'I'll never, ever listen to that stupid little Ginger Mutton and her sock *ever* again!'

'Looks like Ginger's socks-appeal is on the way out,' said Memphis, deadpan.

'She must have gone crazy,' said Sara. 'Or else Carl has. Come on, let's try to find her.'

As it turned out, that wasn't too hard. She was sitting alone in the cloaks in the Humanities block, looking miserable. Even Big Stitch seemed listless and lost on the end of her wrist, his newly repaired tongue hanging out of his wool-rich mouth.

Memphis folded her arms. 'Cass didn't show, huh?'

'She might do,' said Ginger pathetically. 'There's still two-and-a-half minutes left till the end of lunch.' She sighed. 'And after I rushed through all my predictions for Vicki's friends, too.'

'Um, yes, about those predictions . . . ' Sara glanced at Memphis. 'You're still using Carl's cheat-sheet, right?'

Ginger patted her wrist. 'Got it right here. I just hitch up the Stitch when I need a prompt.'

'Well, are you sure you didn't rush through those predictions a little *too* quickly?' asked Memphis. 'Maybe got kind of confused?'

'Huh?' She looked at them blankly. 'I don't get it.'

'Vicki's clone club sure did,' said Sara. 'You told Elise, Denise, and Therese that something nice would happen to each of them, right?'

'Yeah,' said Ginger with a little smile. 'Carl wanted them buttered up and in a good mood before he woos Vicki after registration. What's the problem?'

Sara winced. 'One got drenched, one's a walking doughball, and the other one's half-drowned in manure!'

Ginger jumped up in horror. 'What?'

'It's true,' said Memphis.

'But . . . but how? Why?' croaked Ginger. 'When they tell Vicki, she'll hate me. And when I have to tell her that Sam's not her true love after all, she'll *really* hate me. She'll think I'm a fraud!'

'You *are* a fraud,' Sara pointed out. But Ginger looked as if she was going to cry again, so Sara quickly added: 'Kind of.'

'And you *have* to convince Vicki that Sam's not her true love,' Memphis reminded her. 'Or else Carl will come clean about what he's been up to and *everyone* will think you're a fraud.'

Ginger stared at her in horror, and Sara rolled her eyes. 'Nice pep talk, Memph.'

'Well, don't worry,' said Memphis. 'I've got that part of the problem totally covered.'

Ginger didn't say anything, but her sock nodded feebly.

Then the siren sounded for the end of lunch. Ginger started to tremble. Big Stitch shook with her.

'Come on,' said Sara quietly. 'Let's get this over with.'

Afternoon Registration

It didn't take Sam long to get up to speed on what had gone wrong at lunchtime. The soaking, sticky, smelly Chic Clique made eloquent evidence, perched miserably on their stools and sending evil glares over at Ginger. She sat cowering in the corner, keeping her distance.

'It's official. Carl's gone crazy,' said Sam, as Sara and Memphis stood shielding him from the rather anxious looks that Vicki Starling was sending over. 'Either that or he was trying to get Vicki's gang out of the way so he could make moves on her when no one's around.'

'Well, if that *was* his plan, it hasn't worked out,' said Sara.

'Well, here's *someone* who has!' grinned Sam as Fido staggered in, sweaty, red-faced, and panting for breath. Thomas limped along beside him.

'You worked him tough, huh?' said Sara.

 135

'He's half-killed me,' gasped Fido.

Doubting Thomas smiled. 'I don't believe in half-measures.'

'OK, so he's *totally* killed me.'

'I've worked Fido hard and given him a whole new game plan.'

'Oh yeah?' said Sam. 'What's that—give up before you start?'

'I'm going to fool my opponents into thinking I'm no kind of threat,' panted Fido.

'Shouldn't be hard!' said Sara. 'Now, what about *your* game plan, Memphis?'

'Oh, *that* . . . '

'You'd better be ready,' said Sam nervously. 'Here she comes now.'

Vicki walked over to Sara and Memphis and cleared her throat meaningfully. They moved aside, and Sam felt a twinge of guilt at the hurt expression on Vicki's face.

'You never showed today,' she said stiffly. 'Anything wrong?'

'He was busy with Sara,' said Memphis. 'Didn't you know they were an item?'

Sam froze. Sara's eyes widened.

Vicki stared at her. 'They're a *what*?'

 136

'Sam wanted to let you down gently, but you never took the hint,' said Memphis.

'Is this true, Sam?' said Vicki coldly.

'Er . . . I guess?' Sam croaked, his cheeks flushing scarlet.

Vicki looked at Sara. 'You mean cow. I bet you've been laughing at me all day, haven't you?'

'No!' Sara protested. 'It's not like that—'

Fido had overheard. He staggered up to her, puzzled. 'You're going out with Sam, Sara? Since when?'

Sara opened her mouth but the words wouldn't come. 'Er . . . well . . . I'm not exactly . . . '

'Oh, don't try to deny it now,' stormed Vicki.

Now Fido looked at Sam. 'So *that's* why you didn't care that Vicki was into you!' He stomped back to his seat. 'You could have told me!'

Sam squirmed in his chair as if his bum was chewing a toffee. 'Look, Fido, it's not quite how you—'

'Oh, save the excuses,' said Vicki furiously. 'I'm sure you'll be very happy together, you— you leap year freaks!'

'Well now, that's a bit harsh,' said Sam. 'I mean, I know *Sara's* a bit freakish, but I—'

 137

'This is all down to you, Ginger!' Vicki said, storming over to the timid girl's lonely corner, her Chic Clique following on behind. 'You and your sock have made me a laughing stock!'

'And us!' chorused Denise and Elise.

Therese stamped her foot. 'I was going to say that!'

'I think it's pretty obvious that your sock is just a load of stupid rubbish,' Vicki hissed. 'And I'm going to tell the whole school.'

Ginger cringed. 'Please don't! I—I've got a prediction for you!'

'Like I'd believe you *or* that sock after this!' cried Vicki. 'Whatever gift you had, it's totally history. And that's what *you* are, Ginger Mutton.' She jabbed a finger into the little girl's shoulder. 'History!'

Vicki turned and marched away, eyes mean and narrowed, platinum blonde hair swishing over her crimson cheeks, her ladies at her heels. Fido frowned at both Sam and Sara, then stumbled back to his seat.

'Well,' said Memphis awkwardly. 'I thought that went well.'

'It was a disaster!' hissed Sam.

Memphis shrugged. 'Well, it was always going to be messy.'

'Now we know why you wouldn't tell us your plan, don't we!' said Sara. 'What were you thinking of?'

'It was the only quick way to get Vicki off Sam's back—which *was* the idea, right?' said Memphis coolly. 'If I'd told you sooner it would have spoiled the effect. As it was, that look of horror you gave Vicki was the real deal. You looked totally caught out!'

'That's because we were!' said Sam. Then he blushed. 'Horrified, that is, not caught out. Right, Sara?'

'Right,' she insisted.

'And now Fido's going to think I've been holding out on him,' sighed Sam.

Sara clutched her hair. 'The whole class is going to think we're going out!'

'Oh, they didn't all hear . . . ' said Memphis dismissively.

'Sara and Sam, sitting in a tree,' piped some bright spark behind them, starting a chant. 'K-I-S-S-I-N-G!'

139

Ruthless Cook added her bellow to the chant 'First came love, then came marriage—'

'THEN CAME SAM WITH A BABY CARRIAGE!' yelled the whole class—even Therese, until she noticed that Vicki and her clique had their lips firmly closed.

Sara's face was the definition of suffering.

'So, what's the big deal?' said Memphis, as if she'd heard nothing. 'Tomorrow you can say you've decided to be just good friends.' She looked at them both shrewdly. 'If you want to.'

'Of course we want to!' said Sam.

'Definitely!' Sara added, reddening. Then she sighed. 'Anyway, never mind us.'

'Yeah, poor old Vicki,' said Sam, pulling a face. 'I'm not easy to get over, you know.'

'I'll bear that in mind when I dump you tomorrow,' said Sara drily. 'I was talking about poor Ginger!'

Sam turned and saw Ginger had buried her face in her hands. 'Um . . . well, maybe Vicki will turn to Carl now for a shoulder to cry on, and everyone will be happy.'

'And maybe pigs will fly out of your butt,' said Sara.

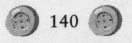 140

Then Penter entered the room. Memphis breezed off to her seat and Sara hobbled along after her.

'Just a moment, Sara,' said Penter. 'Are you limping?'

'Er, yes,' she said, turning to show him her injured knee.

'Good,' hissed Vicki Starling.

'My leg had a disagreement with a trolley,' Sara explained.

Penter looked as if he was about to go *off* his. 'But you're running the girls' hurdles, *and* the fifteen hundred metres!'

'Not any more, sir,' she sighed.

'Lucky for her,' whispered Elise. 'I was going to trip her up.'

'This is a blow to the form, Sara,' said Penter. 'You were a strong contender to win.'

'I've got a problem too, sir,' said Doubting Thomas. 'My ankle. I'm not going to be able to run either.'

'What?' Penter gnashed his yellow teeth. 'But you're the best runner in the form! And I wanted victory. *Victory!*' He paused; seemed to recover himself a bit. 'Victory for the form, I mean.'

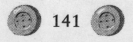

'I've trained up Fido, sir,' said Thomas brightly.

Fido was still panting and wheezing like a chain-smoking pensioner. 'I'm ready to do my bit, sir.'

' "Bit" being the right word,' sighed Penter ungratefully. 'Well, I only hope the rest of you who made the heats are on top form, and that those cheering on are in fine voice. Because if this form doesn't make it into the top three teams overall—everyone's on lunchtime detention for a fortnight!'

A groan went up from the class.

'That's not fair!' complained Ruth Cook.

Penter's thin lips stretched in a smile. 'All's fair in love and sports,' he declared.

And Sam heard Ginger and Vicki speak quietly as one.

'Don't talk to me about love,' they grumbled.

Periods Seven and Eight
Sports Day

An air of gloom had settled upon the class, and as the hooter honked the end of registration, only Penter reacted with decisive action.

'I'm going to find Mrs Hurst and tell her about the dropouts,' he announced. 'Participating athletes will get changed and proceed to the athletes' enclosure. The rest of you will walk in a calm and orderly fashion to the playing fields and congregate by the crash mats. I shall meet you there and personally escort you to your cheering positions.'

'Whoopee,' sighed Sam, as Penter beetled out of the room.

As the rest of the class started listlessly towards the door, Sam spotted Carl Witlow waiting outside. His hair was neatly combed, his shirt was tucked into his scruffy trousers and he was holding a small bunch of flowers.

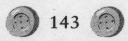

Sam glanced at Sara, and they both winced in advance.

Vicki glared at him as she came through the door. 'What are *you* doing here, you psycho?'

'I . . . I'm—' Carl took in Vicki's angry face and the dishevelled state of her clique and Sam swore he could see the flowers wilting. 'I'm . . . er . . . your true love?'

'You?' laughed Vicki.

Carl looked astounded. 'Well, didn't you hear?'

'Hear what? That you're an ugly, wacko freak? Yeah, I did!' said Vicki venomously. 'You didn't have to come round here to prove it.'

'But . . . but . . . ' Carl stammered. 'But Big Stitch said it was meant to be, right?'

Vicki burst out into mocking laughter. 'Wrong! Even that stupid crummy sock would never predict something as insane as that!' She marched up to him, and Carl dropped the flowers in shock. 'I would never, ever go out with you,' she said, grinding his flowers underfoot. 'Not even if the entire male population was kidnapped by aliens! Not even if my brain was experimented on by mad doctors and I lost my memory, my sanity, and my impeccable sense of good taste! NEVER, EVER, *EVER*. 'K?'

And with that she marched off past him, leaving Carl to weather the sneers and cocked snoots of her clone club and the jeers and laughter of the passers-by. He stood a broken man amid the petals of his trampled flowers while the class trooped past.

Ruthless Cook was bringing up the rear. 'Don't worry about it,' she told Carl. 'Starling's just in a mood over Sam Innocent.' She gave a nasty smile in Sam's direction as she moved off. 'She's still hung up on him, see? Crazy about him!'

Carl glared at Sam. 'Oh she *is*, is she?'

'No way!' Sam protested. 'There's nothing going on—Vicki hates me!' Sam looked around for support, and found Sara, Memphis, and Ginger were the only people still around. 'Have you met my girlfriend, Sara?' he said quickly, slipping an arm around her waist. She squealed and wriggled free. 'She's . . . uh . . . crazy about me.'

'Ginger!' roared Carl. 'What's happening? Why didn't Vicki fall at my feet?'

'She almost threw up on them,' said Sam. 'Does that count?'

'Vicki doesn't believe in Big Stitch any more,' said Ginger sullenly, peering out from behind Sara. 'So there's nothing more you can do.'

He shushed her. 'Don't shoot your mouth off in front of—'

'They already know everything,' she said.

He took a threatening step towards them. 'And *they* told Vicki?'

'We wouldn't waste our breath,' said Memphis.

'It was those stupid predictions you made for Denise, Elise, and Therese,' Ginger complained tearfully. 'They all went wrong!'

Carl bunched up his fists. 'You mean *you* messed them up! Baz was waiting, he said none of them showed up!'

'They showed up and horrid stuff happened!' cried Ginger.

'Baz had arranged flowers for Elise, a chocolate bar for Denise, and perfume for Therese— to get them all supporting your dumb sock!' growled Carl. 'It cost me a fortune, and none of them even showed!'

'I only read what you'd written on the cheat sheet,' said Ginger. 'It's your fault!'

'It is not! It's yours!' yelled Carl. He jabbed

a finger at Sam. 'And it's *your* fault too, you cocky scumball. And *both* of you are going to pay for it.' He stalked off. 'If you're running any races, enjoy them. It's the last time you'll be moving without crutches for a long, long time!'

Sam looked around uneasily at his friends. 'Was that a threat, do you think, or just another random prediction?'

No one bothered to answer.

They headed off to the crash mats together, quickening their step to catch up with the crowds. Once outside they saw that the sky was blue and clear, and while the sun shone brightly there was still a fresh bite to the air.

'Nice day for it,' Memphis remarked.

'What for,' said Sam morosely. 'Getting beaten up?'

Sara dug her elbow in his ribs and gestured to Ginger, who was looking pale and nervous. 'I'm sure Carl's all mouth. He wouldn't dare try anything.'

'He would,' piped Ginger.

This time Sara nudged *her* in the ribs and gestured at Sam.

'It's no good,' said Ginger huskily. 'I can't go through with this. I'm getting out of here.'

Sara frowned. 'But Penter will flip if you don't show up to support the form.'

'Penter won't even notice I'm not there,' sniffed Ginger. 'And the form all hate me anyway.'

'But where will you go?' asked Memphis.

'Somewhere Carl Witlow can't find me,' she said, and darted off like a ginger rabbit into the warren of concrete walkways.

'Wonderful,' said Sam. 'Which leaves Carl with just the one visible target—me!'

'And here's Carl now,' said Memphis, pointing through the noisy clumps of people making their way to the playing fields. 'Looks like he's brought in reinforcements.'

'Baz,' groaned Sam. 'I don't stand a chance!'

'There's only one thing for it, Sam,' said Sara. 'There's only one place where you can be sure they won't get you.'

'Mars?'

'The athletes' enclosure! You'll be safe in there, there are teachers acting as stewards.'

Sam looked at her blankly. 'But I'm not an athlete!'

 148

'Perhaps you should become one,' said Memphis. 'I'll bet Penter needs a volunteer to replace Doubting Thomas.'

'A scrap with Carl and Baz, or running in Sports Day,' Sam sighed. 'I'm not sure which is scarier! You do realize that whenever I get the urge to exercise, I lie down until it goes away?'

'Lie down here and you're going to get trampled,' said Sara. Carl and Baz were getting closer, and neither of them looked happy. 'Go on, move!'

Sam did as he was told, weaving through the crowds at top speed. Within a few moments he began to pant. He wondered if he could start a race of his own, the two hundred centimetres. He was pretty sure he could handle that.

Then he saw that Carl and Baz were racing after him, and he quickened his step.

The athlete's enclosure was a grand name for what was really a strip of field beside the main track, cordoned off with skipping ropes. A few chairs and mattresses had been placed within for the competitors' comfort, and Cabbage Kale the biology teacher stood wary guard over some plastic cups of weak orange squash.

As luck would have it—though whether good

luck or bad luck Sam couldn't quite decide—
Penter was there too, giving a pep talk to his
proud athletes. Vicki, still red-faced, stood close
by with her now-slightly-less-than-Chic Clique.
They studiously ignored him.

'As you know, each of you will be awarded
points according to your finishing position in each
race,' said Penter, turning his red-rimmed eyes on
each of them in turn. 'The form with the most
points overall becomes the gold winner. Now, I
know we're two runners down—and frankly, if
a squad of untrained orang-utans turned up I'd
say they stood a better chance of taking gold. But
if we can win the bronze, I'll be content.' He gave
a nasty smile. 'Remember, my form has featured
in the top three for the last decade. If that record
is broken today—so will you be. Clear?'

'Clear, sir,' came the unenthusiastic chorus.

Baz and Carl were almost on top of Sam now,
cruel smiles playing about their faces. Sam
quickly ducked under the ropes and jogged inside
the enclosure so they couldn't get him.

Penter noticed the movement. 'Innocent, only
athletes may come in here.'

'I know, sir,' said Sam, ignoring the filthy looks

Elise was giving him—though at least now she'd changed out of her uniform and into her PE kit, the rest of her was cleaner. 'But I want to race.'

Penter swung round and stared down at him. '*You*, Innocent?'

He nodded. 'I can't bear to think of your ten-year hold on the Freekham top three coming to an end, sir.'

'I see,' said Penter doubtfully. 'Well, we're desperate, it's true—but I simply don't think you're up to taking Thomas Doughty's place.'

'Give me a chance, sir. I could be your secret weapon.'

'You're sure you know what you're taking on here, Sam?' Penter asked pointedly.

'Oh, yes, sir! I love a challenge, sir.'

'Very well. You're in.'

'Hurrah, sir!'

'In *every single race*, just like Thomas was.'

The smile snagged on Sam's face. 'Ah.'

'I'm sure the rest of the form will find your keenness for such physical punishment with little proper training an inspiration,' said Penter. 'First up is the four hundred metres.'

'Four hundred metres!' gasped Sam.

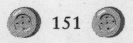

'Is there a problem?'

Sam glanced back and saw Carl and Baz waiting impassively for him.

'No, no problem sir,' said Sam. 'I meant to say, *only* four hundred metres? When do we get on to the real races!'

'The eight hundred and fifteen hundred metres are held nearer the end of the afternoon, when you've had a chance to warm up a bit,' Penter assured him. 'Now, I'll make sure you're added to the official fixtures. You go and find yourself some kit.'

'Yes, sir.' Sam shut his eyes. Talk about out of the frying pan into the fire.

'You can't hide from us for ever, Innocent,' Carl warned him, lurking beside the flimsy skipping rope barrier.

'That's a defeatist attitude, Carl,' Sam called back, taking a few steps closer to where Kale was standing. 'Believe me, I'm going to try!'

As Carl and Baz slouched away, Fido walked up to him, no longer panting like his namesake. 'Problems, Sam?'

Sam half-smiled. 'If *you're* mad at me, yeah.'

Fido shrugged.

 152

'Look, mate, that stuff about me going out with Sara was a load of bog roll,' Sam told him. 'Memphis only said it to get Vicki off my back.'

Fido grinned. 'But why—?'

'It's a long story,' Sam assured him. 'Then again, since it involves a sock or two, maybe *yarn* would be a better word!'

Doubting Thomas came hobbling up. 'Sara told me you need to borrow a PE kit,' he said. 'I didn't believe her.'

'It's true, more's the pity,' said Sam. 'I'm your stunt double, Thomas. I'm taking your place in Sports Day.'

Thomas clearly found this impossible to believe too, but he was too busy laughing to say so.

'They're getting ready for the first race,' said Memphis, staring over at the boys gathering on the track. 'Four hundred metres.'

Sara nodded. 'Poor old Sam's got a real wake-up call coming.'

Rather than risk getting ambushed on his way to the changing rooms, Sam had got changed in

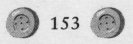

the athletes' enclosure. Luckily for the horrified onlookers, Fido and Thomas had shielded him from view.

'Your boyfriend's a total loser, Knot,' said Ruth Cook, lurking at the back of Penter's cheer squad. 'He's going to come bottom in everything.'

Sara glared at her. 'Well, with a bottom as big as yours, Ruth, I guess you're the expert.'

'I'll kick yours all over this field if you don't—'

'Calm it, girls,' Memphis told them. 'They're under starter's orders.'

'On your marks!' called Mrs Hurst. 'Get set! Go!' She fired the starter's pistol.

To Sara's dismay, Sam pretended he had been shot and staggered about for a while before setting off after the other boys. 'Can I just point out right now that he is no *way* my boyfriend?'

'Yeah, right,' said Ruth.

'He isn't!' she said crossly.

'How about some cheering, ladies,' said Memphis coolly. 'Our boys need inspiring, or we're in for a fortnight of lunchtime detentions!'

Raggedly, self-consciously, Sara and Ruth began urging the boys to get a move on. Sara kept looking around for Ginger, but couldn't see

her. Carl and Baz, on the other hand, were very much in view at the side of the track, jeering and shaking their fists in Sam's direction.

Fido jogged past them, red-faced and panting for breath, Sam a few steps behind him in last place.

'We're *so* doing a fortnight of lunchtime detentions, aren't we?' said Memphis.

'What's up?' gasped Sam as he jogged along behind Fido. They were a good fifty metres behind the opposition.

'Thomas worked me too hard at lunchtime,' Fido panted. 'My legs are killing me!'

'I was relying on you doing well so I could do badly,' Sam complained.

'Sorry to disappoint,' said Fido. 'I'm totally whacked already.'

They limped home to the finish line in a blaze of livid looks and abuse—and no one was jeering louder than Carl and Baz.

Sam tottered into the athletes' enclosure and collapsed on his back, the grass cool against his hot, sweaty skin.

'No time to dawdle, Innocent!' shouted Potter from somewhere close by. 'It's the hundred metre sprint next, then the javelin!'

Sam groaned. 'Getting beaten up has got to be less effort!'

Sara watched Vicki Starling win the girls' 400 metres with ease and Sam come seventh out of eight in the 100 metres—only because one person tripped as they left the starting blocks and never finished. It was the javelin now, and Sam was plodding away to take part. Sara pitied the innocent bystanders nearby.

'Hey, Sara? Sara Knot?'

Sara turned and saw a bucktoothed kid with mousy hair and a centre parting smiling at her hopefully.

'That's me.' She smiled back. 'Who are you?'

'You've been trying to help Ginger, haven't you?' said the girl. 'I'm Beth. Ginger's my friend.' She hesitated, downcast. 'Or she used to be, anyway.'

'What's up?' Sara asked.

'I found this,' said Beth, passing her a bit of

paper. 'I thought you might be able to do something with it.'

With that, the little girl turned and scurried back into the crowd of cheering onlookers.

Memphis peered over her shoulder. 'What is it?'

Sara stared. It was a crumpled scrap of paper, scored with pinholes top and bottom. In spindly blue biro, a number of predictions had been scrawled.

'It's Carl Witlow's cheat sheet,' breathed Sara. 'The scrap of paper Ginger pinned to her sock so she knew what Big Stitch had to say. Look, he's even signed it at the bottom. And here are all today's predictions!'

Memphis took a look. 'Misfortune will befall you, full moon, blah blah blah . . . '

'That was Doubting Thomas's little accident,' Sara confirmed.

'Fido's geography homework gets its mention . . . and look! Denise was supposed to go to the *English* block to find something delicious, not to Home Ec!'

'And you can bet that if she had, she'd have found Baz waiting with her chocolate bar,' said

 157

Sara, snatching back the paper. 'And look. Elise wasn't meant to go to the school farm to find everything coming up roses. She *should* have gone to the top of the school drive. She'd have got her bunch of flowers, not a heap of manure.'

'Probably the same flowers Carl tried to give Vicki,' said Memphis, taking the paper back. 'Yeah, and look here. Therese was supposed to go to the computer room to make a splash with her free perfume.' She frowned. 'Looks like whatever Ginger was reading from at lunchtime, it wasn't Carl's cheat sheet.'

'Of course,' breathed Sara. 'That's why the sock was given back without any fuss. Whoever took it *swapped* the cheat sheet for their own!'

'Makes sense,' Memphis agreed. 'And they changed things round so they could set up *bad* things to happen to Elise and co. But why would Ginger's friend give that to you now? So you can help patch things up between Ginger and the Chic Clique, get her back in favour?'

'I don't know,' Sara admitted, scanning the scribbled words as if some clue might be hidden there.

Then she gasped, and started jiggling about on the spot in excitement.

Memphis frowned. 'You need the loo or something?'

'I just realized. This might be exactly what we need to get Carl off everybody's back, once and for all!' Sara showed the paper to Memphis again. 'Look at his rubbish spelling: Thomas would have *missfortune* coming his way—'

'Whoever *she* is,' joked Memphis.

'And Fido's homework would be the *wurst* in the class.' Sara smacked the bit of paper in triumph. 'I'm sure that those exact misspellings appear in Fido's geography book—in that bit of bogus marking from Killer Collier!'

Memphis nodded slowly. 'So Collier never really saw Fido's work at all! Somehow Carl nicked it off Collier's desk, marked it himself and slipped it back on the "done" pile!'

'And Killer's so scary, Carl could be fairly sure that Fido would be too scared to complain about his lousy grade,' reasoned Sara.

'But how does this help us now?' Memphis wondered.

'Carl's put his name to this note, and he's spelt the same words wrong in Fido's book. If we went to Collier with the evidence that Carl Witlow has been forging his handwriting and marking books . . . '

Memphis grinned. 'Collier would go mental!'

'And Carl would be in ultra-big trouble,' said Sara. 'But if he agrees to let Sam and Ginger off the hook, and crawls back under whatever rock he came out from . . . '

'We keep our mouths shut,' Memphis concluded. 'Brilliant!'

'First, we'd better make sure I'm right. We need Fido's geography book.'

''K. Where's Fido?'

Sara peered about, trying to spot him. 'Over there. Flat on his back on a mattress in the athletes' enclosure.'

'And where's Sam?' asked Memphis.

Sara sighed and shook her head. 'Flat on his face in the long jump sandpit.'

They crossed quickly to the cordoned-off strip.

'Fido!' called Sara. 'I need you, quick!'

'Sara,' said Fido as he clambered up from his mattress, 'you don't know how long I've waited to hear you say that.'

'Ha, ha,' said Sara. 'What I *really* need is your geography book.'

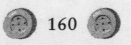 160

'My *what*?'

'Your geography book!' Memphis hollered.

'Why?' asked Fido. 'Want to show a real live E minus to all your friends?'

'Something like that. So can we borrow it?'

Fido made a great show of considering. 'Go on, then. It's in my bag in the boys' changing rooms. Grey hold-all.'

'Can you go get it for us?' asked Memphis.

'Sorry, my big moment's coming up. The hurdles.'

Sara raised her eyebrows. 'After the way you ran the four hundred metres, I bet those hurdles are trembling right now!'

'I've been resting up,' said Fido. 'I feel a bit better. It's Sam who's really in trouble.'

'And speak of the devil,' said Memphis.

Sam came staggering over to them, sweaty and bedraggled with sand in his hair and all over his shoulders.

'How'd you do?' asked Fido.

'Came second in the high jump,' he croaked.

'That's brilliant!' smiled Sara.

'I guess practice makes perfect,' said Sam. 'I've been *for* the high jump so many times . . . '

'How are we doing score wise?' wondered Memphis.

'Somewhere in the middle,' said Fido. '*Lower* middle.'

Sam frowned. 'And how many events have I got left?'

'Eight.'

'Eight?' Sam choked. 'Sara, tell Carl and Baz I've changed my mind. I'll let them duff me up at the time and place of their choosing, and I won't charge travel costs. It's *got* to be better than this!'

'Sam, we might just be able to stop you finding out,' said Sara, slapping him on the back. 'Got to cut and run. Happy hurdling!'

Keeping a careful eye out for teachers—especially Penter—Sara and Memphis sneaked carefully over to the sports hall block.

'I don't see why we couldn't wait till tomorrow,' Memphis complained.

'You saw Carl, he's out for blood,' said Sara. 'We need to deal with this right now. It's not just Sam, it's Ginger too—she's got to show up some time.'

 162

They went in through the main doors and followed the corridor round. The inner doors to the sports hall itself stood open, but a quick check confirmed that the cavernous room was quiet and deserted. Padding quietly onwards, the door to the boys' changing room soon loomed up before them.

Sara found herself whispering. 'I've never been inside the boys' ones before.'

'It's just like ours,' Memphis assured her, with the air of someone who has seen it all. 'Only much, much nastier.' As if to prove the point, she opened the door and a gross smell of sweat and muddy boots wafted out.

'Eeuw!' said Sara. 'Since you're the expert, you can go in. I'll keep watch.'

Memphis vanished inside, while Sara waited tensely. If a teacher came and found them now . . .

She started as she heard the main doors around the corner swing open. Two sets of footsteps sounded heavily on the tiled floor.

Sara opened the door and slipped inside. She found herself in a sinister landscape of smelly shoes, sweaty socks, and crumpled shirts.

'Memphis?' she hissed, holding her nose.

'It's all right, I've found it,' said Memphis, brandishing a pink exercise book with triumph.

'Someone's coming!'

Memphis frowned. 'Let's hope they don't come in here.'

They held their breath.

About two seconds later the door swung open—and Carl and Baz swaggered inside.

'Well, well,' said Baz, his thick, blobby lips twitching into a disgusting smile. 'What have we here? Girls in the boy's changing rooms?'

'So?' Sara tossed her hair and crossed her arms. 'It's just somewhere to bunk off.'

The two boys started walking slowly towards them.

'We heard you shouting to your friend with the dog's name about borrowing his geography book,' said Carl. 'Now, what could you want with that?'

'We . . . er . . . missed class today,' said Memphis, holding the book behind her back. 'We just asked if we could copy his work.'

'What, so you can get an E minus too?' sneered Baz.

'Ginger said you know everything,' said Carl, continuing his slow advance. 'Which means you know that *I* marked that cocky kid's work, not Collier.'

'All right, then—yeah, we do,' said Sara crossly. The boys were getting close now, but she and Memphis held their ground. 'And if you don't leave Sam and Ginger alone, we'll show Collier the evidence and tell him who did it.'

'And he'll slaughter you,' added Memphis.

Baz halted, looked at Carl. 'I told you marking the book was a dumb idea—you left *evidence*!'

'Why should Collier believe that *I* did it?' Carl argued.

'Because of your rubbish spelling,' said Sara. 'It matches the same mistakes in your cheat sheet—signed by you.'

Carl's face darkened and he took a step forwards. 'Give me that book.'

'Duh, how about "no"?' said Memphis.

'You ain't got no choice,' said Carl.

He lunged for her. Memphis leaped back and threw the book to Sara. She grabbed for it—and Baz tried to grab her. She stamped on his foot and he howled with pain.

'Now we're even!' she shouted as she pushed past him.

'Get her!' yelled Carl.

Sara threw open the changing room door and dashed outside into the corridor. Then she hesitated. What if Memphis was in trouble in there, needed her help?

But a moment later, both Carl and Baz burst out. Sara had the book—*she* was their target. She started to run again, past the inner doors to the sports hall, making for the main exit—but her bad leg was throbbing with pain, slowing her down. She gasped as a heavy hand caught hold of her shirt and started dragging her back.

Carl's voice snarled in her ear: 'Give . . . me . . . that—'

'Book!' Memphis yelled from somewhere behind her. 'Quick, Sara!'

Sara tossed the book in a high arc over her shoulder. The same second she tore free of Carl's grip, spun around—and saw that he and Baz were already sprinting after Memphis, who had ducked inside the sports hall.

She followed, gritting her teeth against the pain

in her leg. Memphis was running for the far side of the hall, Carl and Baz hot on her heels.

'Memphis!' she shouted. 'Throw it back to me!'

'Baz, cut off her way out,' said Carl, signalling to the inner doors. 'She mustn't get away with that book!'

Baz nodded and circled around behind Sara, blocking her escape.

Memphis was making for the fire exit. But she couldn't open it. Carl put on a spurt of speed. She turned, saw he was almost on top of her, and hurled the book wildly.

It hit the floor and skidded on the smooth surface.

Sara and Carl both raced from different directions to be the first to grab it. Sara barely beat him to it, gasping for breath. But Baz was racing towards her, his mullet flapping like an ungainly bird.

'Over here!' shouted Memphis desperately.

But as Sara turned to throw the book once more, her bad leg twisted and gave way beneath her. She fell back against a pile of squashy blue crash mats stacked up against the wall.

Carl and Baz loomed up over her.

'Leave her alone!' shouted Memphis.

167

Carl reached down and snatched the book from Sara's grip. With a broad smile at Baz, he opened it, found the offending page, and slowly ripped it out.

Memphis dodged past them and crouched next to Sara. 'You all right?' she panted.

'I'm fine,' she gasped bitterly. 'But we've lost the evidence!'

Carl crumpled the page into a tight ball in his fist.

Memphis hauled Sara to her feet and pulled her away from the crash mats. 'All right, you win,' she said. 'You've got what you wanted. Now leave us alone.'

Carl shook his head. 'You've put us to a lot of trouble. What do you reckon, Baz?'

Baz sneered. 'I reckon we should give them a taste of what we're gonna give Innocent and Ginger.'

Memphis and Sara backed away.

'Look out!' hissed a tiny voice close by.

Sara frowned. It was coming from *behind* the crash mats.

And as Baz and Carl came closer, the crash mats began to topple forwards.

The boys looked up in sudden, silent alarm as a menacing shadow fell over them.

Moments later, with a resounding, echoing smash, the crash mats followed. Carl and Baz were flattened beneath them, their gasps and cries of protest muffled by the thick squashy material. Only Carl's arm protruded from the pile, the precious evidence still balled in one hand.

Sara opened his fingers and grabbed it. 'Ours I think,' she said.

'Thanks to our rescuers,' said Memphis, nodding at the two figures who'd been hiding behind the crash mats, now exposed.

Ginger and Mindy.

Sara grinned madly. 'So *this* is where you got to, Ginge!'

'We were taking some time out to patch up our friendship,' Mindy explained. 'Behind the mats seemed like a good hiding place if any teachers came looking.'

Ginger nodded. 'And get this. I'd like you to meet . . . the socknapper!'

She gestured at Mindy, who blushed faintly.

Memphis stared at her. '*You* took Big Stitch?'

Mindy nodded shyly. 'I only took him because I wanted to stop Ginger making her predictions. But she just made herself a new one instead.'

'Little Knit,' Sara agreed. 'So then, since there was no point holding on to Big Stitch any more, you gave him back—with a forged cheat sheet!'

Mindy looked at Ginger fondly. 'Me and my friends knew she'd never remember the old predictions, so we messed them up a bit.' She gave a surprisingly wicked grin. 'Then we made sure our predictions came true for the Chic Clique.'

'Hey!' moaned Carl from under the mountain of mats. 'These things weigh a ton!'

'Yeah, let us out!' wailed Baz.

'Shut up,' said Memphis. 'We're doing the explanations here.'

'So you sabotaged the sock, Mindy,' said Sara. 'And left Ginger's rep in tatters. But why? Isn't she supposed to be your friend?'

'That's exactly it,' said Ginger. 'Mindy, Beth, Deborah. *They're* my friends, my *real* friends.'

'We were getting tired of the A-crowd treating our mate like a gimmick when she's worth so much more,' said Mindy. 'That's why we picked on the Chic Clique—so Ginger would see how quickly they dumped her once the sock flopped.'

Ginger gave her a tearful smile. 'I've been so stupid, Mindy,' she said. 'I've missed you guys, I really have. But I just had this dumb dream that I could be really popular . . . '

'Duh,' said Sara. 'There are ways of improving your image that don't involve a sock—at least not one on your hand.'

'What are you on about?' said Ginger.

'You're quick on your feet. I saw the way you ran from the bike sheds at lunchtime, and at afternoon reg.' Sara checked her watch. 'So why don't you take my place in the fifteen hundred metres? There should still be time.'

Ginger gulped. 'Run a race?'

Mindy shrugged. 'What have you got to lose?'

'It's what *we've* got to lose if you *don't* run,' added Memphis with a smile. 'Sounds like we're down on points overall—and you know what Penter said about getting into the top three . . . '

'No pressure then,' said Ginger nervously.

'You can do it, Ginge,' smiled Mindy. 'We'll cheer you on!'

 171

'I'll lend you my kit,' said Sara.

'What about *us*?' cried Carl, flailing about but still pinned beneath the heavy mats.

'We've got the evidence back now,' Sara told him. 'So behave yourselves, or else!'

'Yeah, you can just stay away from me from now on, Witlow!' yelled Ginger with sudden anger. 'And if you or your mates try to hurt Sara or Memphis or Sam—or *anyone* I like—then I'll tell the whole school how you two big tough guys were knocked flat by a pair of dweeby little girls. Clear?'

'Clear,' said Carl weakly.

Memphis whistled. 'Who needs hard evidence to keep them in line when we've got Mauler Mutton here!'

Ginger cleared her throat and beamed. 'Ladies—that felt good! And now, if you'll excuse me . . . '

'You've got a race to run,' smiled Sara.

Sam was enduring his final torture: the boys' 1500 metres. His legs felt as weak and wobbly as melted jelly, but they kept cramping up as

if someone was squeezing them with pliers. His breath came in wheezing gasps. He had run, jumped, run, thrown things, fallen over, run, pole-vaulted and smashed into the bar, and run *again*. He had pushed himself over the edge of exhaustion and was ready to flop flat on his face into total fatigue.

But the weird thing was, he was actually starting to enjoy himself.

This was his last race. And the crowd were really cheering him on. He'd come from nowhere and taken part in just about everything except the girls' relay. Sam had always been down on sports, but now, for once in his life, he could appreciate why people did stuff like this. He liked to hear people clapping him. He liked to hear his name being shouted as he went by. And since Carl and Baz were no longer hanging about laughing and jeering every time he got overtaken, his confidence had grown too.

'Last two hundred metres coming up, Innocent!' yelled Mr Penter as Sam ran past. 'Time to sprint! Go, boy, go!'

'I've been, sir!' gasped Sam. 'I went before the shot put, in an empty plastic cup!'

 173

The joke was as tired as he was, but the laughs he got pushed him on. He quickened his ragbag pace to something approaching a sprint. He saw the guy in front, tantalizingly close, if he could just overtake him . . . He ran faster, his feet pounding the grass, his ribs burning and his lungs crackling with every painful breath. But he was gaining ground and dragging himself into third-from-last position. Just a little faster and he might . . . make— No. There was the finish line and he would have to settle for sixth place, and three points. He collapsed to the ground, gasping for air. His race was run. It was all over.

But the applause went on.

Fido and Doubting Thomas came and lifted him between them. Sam gave a regal wave to the people watching. He'd have taken a bow, but knew he didn't have the energy to give it back again.

'I never believed you'd do it!' grinned Thomas as they helped him stumble over to the orange squash stand. 'Every single event! Good going.'

'Not *good*,' Sam corrected him. '*Horrible*.'

'So it is,' murmured Fido.

Sam quailed to see Horrible Hayes was now on drink-serving duty.

'A good effort, Innocent,' said Hayes grudgingly, handing him a drink with a small smile. 'Good enough, in fact, to spare you your after-school detention.'

Sam's jaw dropped. 'You mean it?'

'I only wish you would put the same energy and spirit into my lessons as you do into your sports.'

'Well, sir,' said Sam once he'd drained his drink. 'I'm never, ever going to run again, so that energy and spirit has to go somewhere, doesn't it?'

'See that it goes somewhere productive, boy,' Hayes warned him.

Sam turned and gave a conspiratorial smile to his friends. 'Yeah, as if!'

'Well, you may have got yourself out of one detention,' said Fido. 'But you couldn't save us from another ten from Penter.'

Sam stared in despair. 'There's no way we can make bronze?'

'Doubt it,' said Doubting Thomas. 'Even if Vicki Starling comes first in the fifteen hundred, we'll be two points short.'

'Wait a minute,' said Sam, raising a weary arm to point. 'Do you see what I see?'

'It's a mirage,' said Fido.

'A *Mutton* mirage!' Thomas confirmed.

There was Ginger, in a PE kit way too big for her, stepping up to the starting line.

'A late entry for the race,' called Sara, grinning and waving from the side of the enclosure.

Fido grabbed Sam's shoulder. 'With Ginger running too, we might just make it!'

'I don't believe that for a minute,' said Doubting Thomas.

'So did you get my geography book?' Fido called.

Sara seemed to find this funny. 'Eventually.'

'And did you find it useful?'

'You have no idea,' she assured him.

'Get over here, Sam,' Memphis called. 'You'll never guess what's been going on . . . '

The starter's pistol went off. Ginger set off at a gallop, and Memphis's mouth started moving ten to the dozen.

Sam listened as she and Sara told their story, marvelling at what they'd been up to. But as the laps went by, Sam found his attention gradually shifting on to Ginger. Slowly, steadily, the opposition was starting to flag. But Ginger was keeping up her pace. She took sixth place. Then fifth. Then fourth . . .

Sara trailed off from the victorious conclusion of her tale as Vicki Starling launched into a spirited sprint for the final stretch. Of course she did—she was Vicki Starling, winning came naturally. But Ginger was building up speed too, working her skinny legs, pumping her weedy arms up and down until with a Big Stitch-style squawk she overtook another runner to breast the tape in third place.

'Yes!' whooped Sara, and Memphis punched the air.

'She did it!' gasped Fido. 'Ginger actually did it!'

'We've got the bronze!' grinned Sam. 'And got out of detention!'

Doubting Thomas shook his head in a daze. 'I just can't believe it!'

Ginger stared around at the cheering crowd incredulously. Mr Penter gave her two thumbs up. Even Vicki Starling gave her a pat on the back that didn't seem *too* patronizing.

But taking pride of place among those cheerers was a bundle of geeky looking girls and boys, led by Mindy and Delhi, dancing and jiggling at the front. They weren't just celebrating a race well won, but the return of a friend to the fold.

HOMETIME

'You know,' said Sam. 'Despite everything, this has been a good day.'

Sara looked down at her bruised leg ruefully and shuddered at her near misses in the sports hall. But she knew what Sam meant.

They were hanging out on the grass at the top of the school drive with Memphis, watching the crowds drift home. Two faces they knew wouldn't be passing were those of Carl and Baz.

'Such a shame Hurst found them in the sports hall, still trying to wriggle out from under those mats,' said Memphis, her sea-green eyes sparkling.

Sara nodded. 'And, of course, they couldn't say how they wound up there, so she thought they were just mucking about and gave them detentions!'

'Who says there's no justice in the world?' said Sam, smiling.

'Fido,' Sara reminded him. 'He lent us his

geography book from the kindness of his heart, and we turned it to pulp.'

'Since it's you, he won't stay mad for long.'

'Since it's me, he's already forgiven me.' Sara stuck her tongue between her teeth. 'No one minds losing an E minus. Anyway, I've convinced him to copy out the essay again and hand it in for re-marking.'

'Re-markable,' smiled Sam.

'Hey, here's the girl of the match.' Sara started waving. 'All right, Ginger?'

Ginger came up to them, red-cheeked and grinning. 'Hey! How's it going?'

'I should be able to walk again,' said Sam. 'After several weeks' intensive bed rest.'

'You saved Penter's reputation *and* our necks, Ginge,' said Sara. 'The whole class will be wanting to thank you.'

Ginger shrugged shyly. 'I guess.'

Mindy nodded. 'What you did was really cool. And you did it without your sock puppets!'

'Well . . . ' Ginger looked at them guiltily. 'Actually, that's not strictly true.'

Sara frowned at her. 'Don't tell me Big Stitch *told* you you'd come third!'

 180

'No, nothing like that,' said Ginger. 'I mean I wore Big Stitch on one foot, and Little Knit on the other!' She pointed out her mismatched socks sticking out from her trainers. 'You see? They really *are* special socks!'

Sam gave her a look. 'Just keep them on your feet for a while, OK?'

'Hey, Ginge,' someone called. It was Cassie Shaw.

Ginger gave her an awkward smile. 'Hey, Cassie.'

'I couldn't make it at lunchtime,' she said. 'You know how it is. Maybe you could do your sock routine for us tomorrow at break instead?'

Ginger bit her lip. 'Tomorrow break?'

Mindy looked at her hopefully.

'Sorry, Cass,' said Ginger. 'I've got plans tomorrow. Maybe some other time, 'K?'

Cassie's mouth hung open and she took a step back as if she'd been slapped in the face. 'Whatever,' she said icily, and stalked off down the drive.

'Yay!' cried Mindy, punching the air.

'Whatever else Big Stitch tells me,' said Ginger firmly, 'I'm going to keep it to myself.'

Mindy slipped her arm in hers. 'Come on, Ginge. Let's go to my place. We can eat ice cream and play Xbox . . .'

'See you, guys,' called Ginger, as they walked off together down the drive.

'Did you check Cassie's face just then?' laughed Memphis. 'The geek strikes back. That was priceless!'

'Score one to Ginger!' Sam agreed.

'But it looks like Ice-Queens United might be wanting to equalize,' Sara warned him. 'Here comes Vicki and co.'

'Leave this to me,' said Sam.

He walked painfully over to where Vicki and the Chic Clique were waiting on the pavement.

'You OK?' Vicki asked him, arms folded tightly across her chest.

'Just about,' he shrugged. 'Are you?'

'I overheard what you told Fido in the athletes' enclosure, Sam,' said Elise. 'About only pretending to go out with Sara to put Vicki off.'

'Oh,' said Sam. 'You did, huh?'

Vicki nodded. 'And she told me. I guess you must think I'm pretty stupid.'

'Pretty, yes,' said Sam smiling. 'But not stupid.'

 182

Vicki smiled back. 'At least I've learned that letting a sock decide your love life isn't the greatest idea in the world.'

'We all have to find our own fate,' said Elise.

'Like, totally,' agreed Denise.

'I was going to say that,' Therese complained quietly.

'No hard feelings?' said Sam, offering his hand to Vicki.

She shook it briefly, and half-smiled. 'See you around, Sam Innocent.'

'Till proved guilty,' he called after her, as she and her girlie gaggle moved off down the drive.

'Made up?' Memphis enquired.

'Made up that it's all over, yeah!' said Sam.

'And we don't have to pretend we're going out any more!' said Sara. 'So all's well that ends well!'

'Well, I'll just let you broken-hearted lovebirds say your last goodbyes,' said Memphis, with a wink. 'I'm out of here. See ya!'

They waved her off. Sara felt in her pocket for Carl's cheat sheet, ready to rip it in two as a final farewell to the day's sock-infested events.

But as she scanned over the list of prophecies, she paused.

'What's up?' asked Sam.

'Carl's list of bogus predictions,' she said. 'The one about sending Leslie to the sports hall is here, but the one about sending me to the caretaker's hut isn't—so why did she get the two prophecies confused?'

'She was probably talking out of her hat as well as her sock,' Sam suggested.

'Come on,' she said, heading off to the caretaker's hut, a strange sense of destiny coming over her.

'So this is where your good luck's supposed to happen?' said Sam doubtfully once they'd arrived. 'Maybe she meant you'd get to hang here with me —a lot of girls would think themselves *very* lucky.'

She gave him a withering look and started to search the long grass that had grown up around the hut.

And in the very first place she looked, she saw a silver glint among the green.

'Sam,' she breathed, a shiver running through her. 'Sam, it's my bracelet! The one I lost last week . . . I looked everywhere for it. And here it is— right where Ginger meant to say I'd find good luck!'

'Could she have nicked it?'

'No way. I lost it at home, Sam. My dad accidentally threw it out with some rubbish!'

'Really?'

'Really.'

Sam straightened up. 'Then it's true.'

'What's true?'

'That there are more things in heaven, Earth, and the laundry basket than are dreamt of in your philosophy,' he said impressively. 'That's Shakespeare, that is.'

'Rewritten by Sam Innocent?'

He shrugged. 'I may have made some small improvements. Basically it means, "Loads of freaky weird stuff happens and we just don't get it . . . " '

'We get it here all right,' said Sara, happily slipping on her long-lost bracelet. 'If it's weird stuff you want, you'll find it at Freekham High— any day of the week!'

Steve Cole spent a happy childhood being loud and aspiring to amuse. At school his teachers often despaired of him one of them went so far as to ban him from her English lessons, which enhanced his reputation no end.

Having grown up liking stories, he went to university to read more of them. A few years later he started writing them too. Steve has also worked as a researcher for radio and an editor of books and magazines for both children and adults. *One Weird Day at Freekham High: Sock* is his second novel for Oxford University Press.